A gaunt, bent-over figure dimly glimpsed in the dusk

That's all the man was. He walked the same route through the same neighborhood every day for five years. Yet the people who lived there knew nothing about him. He never stopped, rarely spoke.

Then one night he failed to appear. The people in the area were worried. They had grown used to the mystery man. So they searched for him.

And found out the terrible truth about the gaunt scarecrow who had haunted their streets.

THE
Limits of
PAIN

K Arne Blom

A RAVEN HOUSE MYSTERY FROM
W🌐RLDWIDE

TORONTO · LONDON · NEW YORK

Raven House edition published February 1981
First printing September 1980

ISBN 0-373-60027-5

THE MAN

THEY PUT THE CALL THROUGH to his room.

"Hello, yes? This is Lund Police, Crime Division."

"Oh, good afternoon. I'm sorry to trouble you. But it's about a murder."

The words made him drop his cigarette onto the floor. He leaned forward and swiftly picked it up again.

"Murder?"

"Yes. I've killed my wife. I'd be grateful if you or someone else would come here and, er, take over, sort of... everything."

Martin Holmberg stubbed his cigarette out in the ashtray and ran his hand across his forehead. Disturbed people phoning the police to give themselves up for something they hadn't done, or something they deep down wished to do, were not common, but such calls did happen occasionally.

There was something in the man's voice that made him take it seriously, a fundamentally melancholic matter-of-factness, a kind of sorrowful, resigned verification.

"Who am I speaking to?" said Martin Holmberg.

"My name is August Hermansson. What is yours?"

The question was as astounding as it was logical.

"Holmberg. Martin Holmberg. I'm a C.I.D. inspector. You say you've killed your wife. Why?"

"If you'd be so kind as to come here, we could talk about it. I... I could do with some help... some help with a few things. Practical things... and...."

Martin was astonished by the calmness of the man's voice. "Where are you speaking from?" he asked.

"Home, of course. Where else?"

"What is your address?"

"I live on Broad Street."

"The number?"

He was told, and wrote it down on a piece of paper.

"Listen," said Martin Holmberg. "I'll come to your place at once. Stay where you are. Don't touch anything. Leave everything alone. Sit down on a chair and wait until I come. How did you kill her?"

"I cut the arteries of both wrists."

Martin closed his eyes and swallowed.

"I see," he said. "Now keep calm. I'll be with you as soon as I can. Wait for me."

"Yes, of course." The man's voice sounded slightly surprised. "Of course I'll wait for you. Why shouldn't I? If I wasn't going to do that, I wouldn't have phoned you."

Martin put the receiver down and ran his hand across his mouth. The other went out toward the cigarette packet to the left of his desk. He put a cigarette in his mouth and pressed a number combination on the intercom.

"Order duty officer speaking."

"Hello, Martin Holmberg here. Can you send a patrol to Broad Street at once. I've just had a call from some lunatic who says he's cut his wife's wrists."

"Oh, hell! What number?"

Holmberg told him, adding, "Ask the boys to wait down on the street until we come. I don't know what kind of creature this is—whether he's armed or what he might get up to. His name's August Hermansson. Lives on the third floor. They could take a look to see if anyone of that name does live there. It could all be a hoax."

"Okay. We've dealt with that sort of loony before."

"Thanks. See you."

He lighted the cigarette and went out into the corridor. The door to Seved Olofsson's room was ajar and he pushed it open. The room was empty.

Hell, thought Martin and went across to Leif Mansson's door, which was closed. He drummed a swift signal on it and opened the door. Mansson looked up at him. He was sitting on his chair with his sockless left foot drawn up. He was cutting his toenails.

"God, you almost scared me," he said.

"Get your shoes on," said Martin. "We've got to go out. Bring your gun, too, to be on the safe side."

"What the hell's happened?"

"I'll tell you in the car. Hurry."

Mansson drove. They went under the railway bridge at West Toll, swung to the left and continued along Station Street.

"He sounded tired," said Martin. "And old, I thought. But I might have imagined that."

"Well, it's nice of them to phone and tell us when they've done it," said Leif, dryly factual. "Saves us a hell of a lot of trouble trying to find them."

"You could look at it that way, yes," said Holmberg. "Hope to God he doesn't start shooting the place up when we get there."

"Perhaps we ought to put our bulletproof waistcoats on?" said Mansson.

"They're so difficult to move quickly in. What a hell of a wind," he said unexpectedly.

It was Friday, November 12, 1977. It was more than windy, too; a gale was on the way. The violent gusts hurtled along the streets with ferocious fury, black clouds appearing, forecasting rain. It was two o'clock in the afternoon.

A patrol car was parked by the pavement outside the block, two uniformed policemen standing beside it looking rather lost. Passersby looked curiously at them. Some had gone up to them to ask what was going on, but they had been waved on and told to disappear.

"Someone called Hermansson lives on the third floor," said the elder of the two policemen to Holmberg.

His name was Stig Rosen. He was a short, fair-haired, round-faced man, with a small nose and full lips. Holmberg knew him, but he couldn't remember the name of the younger man with him. He looked so young and confident that he must be one of the new ones, so unsure of himself and the situation that he didn't know what to do with himself. He fidgeted with his shoulder belt and drew his gun.

"Put that away," said Holmberg, then turned to Rosen. "Have you been up to have a look?"

"No, there's a list of tenants on the notice inside the entrance hall. A. Hermansson, it says. I think it's that guy staring at us up there."

Mansson and Holmberg looked up in the direction of his pointing thumb.

A face was cautiously peering behind a curtain. They could neither make out the man's features nor get any impression of his age, nor decide whether he was calmly waiting for their arrival or planning something the consequences of which were impossible to foresee.

"What do we do?" asked the young uniformed man.

"What's your name again?" said Holmberg.

"Berfing."

"Do as we tell you," said Holmberg, nodding encouragingly. "There's nothing to get nervous about."

"I'm not nervous," said Berfing sullenly.

"If you aren't, then you shouldn't have become a policeman."

He pretended not to notice the young policeman's flushed face and trembling mouth about to protest, and turned to Rosen again.

"Perhaps we ought to call an ambulance?" he suggested.

Rosen nodded. "Do that, Berfing," he said.

"Should we evacuate the building before we do anything?" said Mansson.

He sounded almost hopeful, as if looking forward to a gun battle and commando tactics and tear-gas bombs. He was one of the uncompromising kind, regarding himself as a front-line soldier in the war against crime and criminals. He had held that view from the day he had entered the police force, and all his years of service, his experience and the maturity of increasing age had not changed his attitude.

Holmberg looked up at the third-floor window, trying to see the man behind the windowpane and make out his features.

He started.

The man had raised his hand.

He was waving.

He was leaning close to the window and looking straight at Holmberg, his expression slightly uncertain and questioning.

"No," he said. "Wait here. I'm going in."

'Alone?' said Mansson, frowning.

Martin Holmberg nodded, looking up at the window again, about to wave back. But the man's face had vanished.

"Alone, ' he said, walking toward the door.

He opened it and went inside. He looked at the list of tenants

Yes, as Rosen had said, third floor. A. Hermansson. And why shouldn't it be as Rosen had said?

He started walking up the stairs. His heart was thumping and it almost seemed as if the beating of his heart was echoing in the stairwell, but then he realized it was his footsteps.

One floor up now.

He went on, clenching and unclenching his hands, feeling

how sweaty they were, feeling his shirt sticking to his back, his armpits sticky with sweat.

Should have taken my overcoat off, he thought.

Two floors up.

Only fourteen stairs left.

He put his hand into his coat pocket and felt the butt of his gun warm from lying in there. His hand closed around it. He kept his hand in his pocket.

He went on, pressed close to the wall.

Twelve steps left, eleven, ten, nine.

He stopped.

"Hermansson!" he said loudly.

The name bounced off the stairwell walls. He saw three closed doors on the landing up there.

Hermansson's door was the one straight ahead.

He took the last stair in one leap, rushed over to the wall beside the door and leaned his back against it.

He was taking deep breaths, trying to control his breathing. He heard steps on the stairs and saw Mansson stick up his head, then Rosen. They had guns in their hands.

Holmberg frowned, but then he drew another deep breath and smiled gratefully at them.

Of course it was utterly insane of him to have come on up quite alone with no backup. No one would thank him for getting himself shot or knifed or having a bomb thrown at him.

But there had been something in the man's voice that had appealed to him, and when he had seen the face in the window, he had sensed that the man simply wanted the help he had asked for.

Mansson and Rosen were lying on the stairs, trying to make themselves as invisible as possible, pressing themselves flat down on the steps.

That can't be all that comfortable, thought Martin.

Then he stretched out his hand and rang the doorbell. A shrill hollow signal rang on the other side of the door, the door immediately opened and Martin found himself looking straight into August Hermansson's eyes.

He nodded.

"I'm Holmberg," he said.

"Thank you for coming," said Hermansson. "She's . . . she's in there. In the bed."

His voice was beginning to betray him, but he swallowed, and straightening up, he met the policeman's eyes.

The man in the doorway who had telephoned to say that he had killed his wife looked all of ninety years old. His thin skimpy hair was chalk white, his face thin and deeply lined. There was a cold gleam of life in his eyes. His body was thin, his fingers long, his hands trembling.

Holmberg saw that the man had blood on his hands and on the gray cardigan buttoned almost up to his neck.

"Wait here," he said. "Wait here."

He moved the old man gently aside with careful hands and stepped into the apartment.

The first thing that struck him was the smell, a close, stifling, moist smell of old dust, old dirt, old furniture, old books, old carpets, old curtains, old clothes. The smell of old age.

He heard the hard heavy raindrops being hurled against the window by the wind outside.

2

THE OTHER MAN

THERE WAS NOTHING VERY SPECIAL about Maria Street in Himmelsholm. It happened to be long, but it wasn't the longest street in the town. It began down by the police station, ran alongside the park where the bird pond was, continued toward the church, then ran into the parallel trunk road. There was nothing special about the street, lined as it was with both old and new apartment blocks, in an area just bordering on the actual center of the town.

And yet there *was* something special about the street.

The man was in Maria Street.

Everyone who saw him simply called him the man. No one knew who he was, but quite a number had seen him. Night after night at exactly the same time. No one really knew what he was up to.

The fact was that he was up to nothing. He was just there. Perhaps it was just this that made people become curious. Some people must have felt some uneasiness, perhaps even fear.

Sooner or later, the man simply had to *do* something. He couldn't go on just being there.

Quite when it had all begun, no one really knew. Anyhow, no one could now remember the first time he had appeared. Perhaps someone or some people had seen him, but then they hadn't thought so much about his being there.

As time went by, more and more people began to wonder what on earth he was doing and why. Doing nothing. Just standing there.

He came, appeared, at the same time. Night after night, regardless of the weather. He stood there on the same corner, night after night, always for the same length of time, then vanished somewhere. No one knew where.

Werner Soderstrom lived with his wife, Lisa, in a three-

room apartment on the corner of Maria Street and Post
Street. They had lived there since March, 1970.

The evening of December 10, 1972, was windy and cold
and showery, that peculiar winter when the snow refused
to lie faithfully white as it usually did in Himmelsholm in
the winter. Werner had gone over to the window and
looked out, down at Maria Street, and he had seen a man
walk past, but he hadn't thought about it.

Three evenings later, he had switched off the television at
ten past ten, yawned and stretched, then gone over to the
window. Lisa was out at a church choir practice and was expected home any minute now. Werner had looked out,
down toward Maria Street, seen a car driving by and a man
walking along the opposite pavement.

He had thought there was something familiar about the
man.

Suppose I've seen him before somewhere, he thought.

Five minutes later, Lisa came back and Werner thought
no more about the matter. That night.

The day before Christmas Eve, Lisa was on her way out to
the butcher's farther down Post Street to fetch the
Christmas ham the shop had promised would be ready at
about midday. On her way down the stairs, she saw the door
opening in G. Malmborg's apartment.

G. Malmborg's first name was Gerd, and she was a
seventy-year-old widow who lived alone in her little apartment consisting of one room, a kitchen, a bathroom, and a
hall so small that two people could hardly stand in it at one
time.

Gerd Malmborg would be seventy-one in February and
seldom had visitors. Very seldom. Neither did she have any
children who might neglect going to see their mother. Her
marriage in that respect had been fruitless.

Lisa saw her coming out onto the landing carrying her
rubbish bag in her hand. She watched her going over to the
rubbish chute and opening it.

"Good morning, Gerd," said Lisa.

Gerd gave a surprised little start.

"Oh, you frightened me!"

"Did I? So you're throwing out your rubbish, are you?"

It was an idiotic question. But Lisa always tried to find
something to say when she came across Gerd, which she
was always doing. Gerd was the kind of lonely person who
invented an errand to the rubbish chute as soon as she

heard footsteps on the stairs, in the hope of exchanging a few words.

Gerd's rubbish bags were without exception remarkably small.

"Yes," said Gerd. "You have to do a bit of cleaning up for Christmas, don't you?"

"Are you expecting someone for Christmas, Gerd?"

"No. Who do you think would come and see an old thing like me?"

"Your family? You must have some family, Gerd."

"We never had any children, the old man and me. Most of the family was on his side, and they don't bother about me now he's gone. My sister's older than me and she lives too far away to come here, poor old thing. And I'm not that mobile myself these days. But . . . how shall I put it . . . have you seen him?"

Lisa frowned and looked questioningly at Gerd.

"Him?"

Had the old girl started imagining things again?

The year before she had managed to confuse the whole stairway by talking about someone who was terrorizing her by ringing her doorbell and then vanishing before she had time to open it.

No one else had experienced this mysterious doorbell ringing. They promised Gerd they would keep their eyes and ears open. So whenever a doorbell was heard to ring in the stairway, they all took note and listened for steps running away. No one ever heard any. But Gerd's complaints about the mysterious ringing on her bell went on.

People listened and heard doorbells ring, but never anyone running away.

An explanation of it all was forthcoming when the man in the apartment next to hers determined to solve the mystery. He simply sat and kept watch just inside his own front door, waiting for the doorbell to ring. His patience was rewarded. The second evening, the bell on her door rang and he flung open his door just in time to see Gerd's front door swiftly closing.

He looked at it with a frown, then it suddenly opened and there was Gerd, staring at him.

"Someone rang it again," she complained when she saw the man. "Was it you?"

"No, Gerd," sighed the man.

They realized that she simply wanted to draw attention to

herself, a symptom of her chronic loneliness, her way of
saying, here I am, bother about me, speak to me.

They hadn't the heart to be annoyed with her.

But now Lisa wondered whether she was cooking something up again.

"Which *him*?" she asked.

"The man down on the street," said Gerd, screwing up
her eyes. "He looks so mysterious. He comes night after
night. At exactly the same time. Haven't you really ever
seen him?"

"No, I haven't," said Lisa. "What's so mysterious about
him?"

"Lisa, dear, you must see that it's not right. There's something very peculiar about a person who walks along the
opposite pavement every single night, always at exactly the
same time, and then exactly twenty minutes later walks
back again."

"Perhaps he goes and buys something at the kiosk along
there."

"Night after night? No, Lisa, dear. There's something
peculiar about that man, you mark my words."

"Yes, well, perhaps there is. What does he look like?"

"Well, it's not easy to see, but he looks like most people.
He sort of sneaks along the opposite pavement. It's difficult
to see what he looks like. But look for yourself tonight and
you'll see. At ten to ten he comes, walking in the direction
of the church. Then he's gone for a while. And on the dot of
ten past ten he's back again, walking in the other direction."

"I will, I'll have a look," said Lisa. "I must go now."

"Don't forget now. Ten to ten. And then twenty minutes
later. Don't forget to look."

"All right, I won't," said Lisa.

But then she didn't give the matter another thought.

THE NIGHT BEFORE CHRISTMAS EVE, Werner was watching
television and Lisa was making herring salad in the kitchen,
pickling herrings, fixing the Christmas fish, preparing the
rice and other small culinary matters.

At ten o'clock an invisible and irrational force seemed to
call Werner. He didn't know why, but he suddenly got up,
went across to the window and looked out.

It was pouring with rain outside and there was an inhos-
pitable wind. Truly foul weather, not like Christmas in the

old days, with the snow white and clean, the air pure and fresh; when it was crisply cold and the skies were high, making breathing a pleasure; when life looked like an inviting, peaceful and benevolent Christmas card, with only the little Christmas gnomes missing.

Those were the days.

Werner stood there looking out. A few cars went by and it was dark and drab out, the long green fence on the opposite side of the street looking black.

Then he saw the man.

Werner glanced down at his watch. Nine and a half minutes past ten. He wondered if his watch was slow.

"Lisa!"

"Yes, what is it?"

"Come and look. Quick!"

She came in swiftly.

"What is it? What're you doing over there?"

"Come and look. Down there on the pavement across the road. Do you see that man there?"

"Him . . . yes."

They stood watching him in silence.

Then Werner told her about his previous observations of the man.

"It must be the man Gerd was talking about."

"What?"

Lisa told him.

"My God," said Werner. "I wonder what kind of person he is. He doesn't look peculiar in any way."

It was so dark, it was almost impossible to see him clearly. But he walked leaning slightly forward as if almost shuffling along, and he seemed well wrapped up.

Although there was no snow, it was cold outside.

"I wonder where he goes?" said Werner quietly.

"I suppose it's nothing to do with us," said Lisa.

"No, but I was just wondering."

THE WHOLE BLOCK seemed to know about the man by Christmas. Gerd had seen to it that the word had spread. And as it was a stairway where people knew each other and talked to each other, even those Gerd hadn't told, or had not had an opportunity to tell, knew all about the man who appeared night after night and then vanished again.

Thus it came about that all the people living on that stairway who had not gone away for Christmas were standing at their windows facing Maria Street at ten to ten, and they all saw the man come from the south and walk northward out of their field of vision.

He came on Christmas Eve, too, and again they were faithfully standing there waiting. At ten past ten they saw him coming from the north and vanishing southward.

By the time New Year's Eve came along almost the whole block knew the man. The word had spread to the other stairways.

While that spring came and went, it was as if the people who lived in that long block with its five stairways had an enigma in common. People who had previously never even nodded to each other stopped and began talking about him.

Someone suggested they should phone the police, but the suggestion, whether seriously meant or not, was quickly voted out of court.

One couldn't do that. The man hadn't done anything. He hadn't done anyone any harm.

But they did know where he went now.

He stopped on the corner of Maria Street and Merchant Street, then just stood there, apparently looking straight ahead, until punctually like a clock he suddenly, without further ado, turned on his heel and slowly made his way back.

ONE NIGHT IN JANUARY, 1975, he didn't come. That made people begin to wonder. They talked about what might have happened. But they soon calmed down, because the next night he was back again. And the next night.

So night was added to night, week to week, month to month, and even year to year, and it became 1977. The man came just as regularly.

But people didn't talk about him anymore, or stop to discuss the man when they met. They knew he was there now, and that was enough. He belonged there, had become something on the inventory.

Of course, he was a mystery.

Of course, they still wondered equally inquisitively just who he was, where he came from, where he went back to, and why he stood there on the corner.

But for some fundamental reason these were questions to which they did not want to know the answers. That would have spoiled something they could not define.

The man and his puzzling circumstances became a kind of security.

Then came December of this year, 1977, and on the fifteenth the man deserted them. They expected him to come back on the sixteenth, but he didn't. The man they had got so used to that they could set their watches by him did not come on the seventeenth, either.

When he did not appear on the eighteenth, active interest in his existence began to revive again. People began to talk about him.

They were all intrigued by the mystery of why he had disappeared, for that he clearly had.

He did not come on either the nineteenth or the twentieth.

They discussed uneasily what might have happened to him, if anything *had* happened, which it looked as if it had, or else he would have, wouldn't he?

Two days before Christmas Eve, after mature consideration and what he regarded as obstinate nagging from his wife, Lisa, Werner Soderstrom decided to go to the police.

He went on behalf of a great number of people.

They simply had to know why the unknown man had suddenly vanished like that.

THE MAN

"THE PROSECUTOR SAYS it's impossible," said Seved Olofsson. "However much he would like to himself, he says it's unthinkable."

Holmberg shoved his chair back and put his feet up on the edge of his desk.

"No," he said. "Of course, I can see that. I hadn't expected anything else, really. But it's bloody awful all the same. What's the point? He didn't do it with any ill intention. He did it out of love."

"Hell, I know that. So does the prosecutor. But that doesn't help, does it?"

"Then think of his age. I mean, hell, they can't send him to prison, can they? He's eighty-seven years old!"

"Mercy killing is against the law," said Seved.

"You don't have to defend the law," snapped Martin. "The prosecutor does enough of that."

"I'm not defending it," said Seved, then fell silent.

He stared down at the floor, tugging at his bright red beard, looking thoughtful.

"I presume," he went on after a while, "that there are people who commit so-called mercy killings and never come before the courts?"

"Of course there are. I know at least two doctors here in town who have switched off the respirator. The patients were utterly hopeless cases, their brains dead but their hearts still beating. The only point in keeping them alive would have been for scientific reasons—so that medical science could find out how the organs functioned. I saw a ward of respirator cases once."

Martin shook his head.

"It was inhuman," he went on. "Three of them, lying there in their beds, dead. But their hearts were beating, thanks to all that bloody apparatus. Their reactions were minimal and they had no contact with life whatsoever. But the machines were keeping them alive. Respirators and drip tubes and defecation tubes and God knows what other tubes. I'm sure they weren't suffering. Well, I imagine not. But it must have been sheer hell for their families."

"But they'd only just discovered she had cancer. She could have lived for a few years."

"Lived?" exclaimed Holmberg. "What kind of life would that have been? And what kind of life do you think that would have been toward the end? When the pain started and she would be screaming for a morphine shot to be able to endure it. I don't call that living. And she was old, too."

"I know someone whose father is ninety-seven. Last year he gave up smoking because he was convinced smoking was damaging his health. He'd been smoking since he was fifteen."

Holmberg did not laugh.

"I'd better go and talk to him at once."

"Is he still living at his apartment?"

"Yes. What's on your mind?"

"It can wait until you get back. We'll have to have a briefing with the whole division. It's about a terrorist they think might be in town."

"Who thinks so?"

"Them in Stockholm."

"Oh, God. Can't they do that themselves?"

"You'd think so. When do you think you'll be back?"

"Give me an hour. Or two. Then I'll have time to buy some Christmas presents. I haven't got all the things for the kids yet."

"In working hours?"

"Yes. When the hell can I do it otherwise?"

IN TWO DAYS' TIME it would be Christmas Eve.

It was clearly going to be a white Christmas this year, too, like the year before. Then it had snowed heavily and the white blanket had remained over Lund, not thawing as usual in the south generally and in Lund in particular.

This time last year, Martin had gone into town on the bus with his six-year-old daughter, Inger, to buy a new base for their Christmas tree. Their old one leaked. The sidewalks and stores were crowded with jostling people, and Martin, a practical-minded man who presumed Kerstin would have probably forgotten to buy all sorts of things for Christmas, had spent the next three hours in five stores.

Does every single idiot in town do his Christmas shopping this late, he thought.

With his hot and wriggling little daughter whining and fretting, and hardly able to stand any longer, he had come out of the last shop so loaded with parcels that he was unable to carry her, too.

"Can't we take a taxi?" she said.

She liked taxis more than anything else, but they were horribly expensive. Not so easy, either, finding a taxi in Lund when you most needed one. Before Christmas like this, it was quite impossible.

So they had gone home on the bus.

The bus was crowded with people armed with so many parcels and carrier bags that the general impression was one of Santa's sledge.

At last they had reached their stop and at last they had managed to push their way off the bus, arriving hot, sweaty and tired.

Martin lived on the very eastern outskirts of Lund, in a new town house. They had moved there a few years before from an apartment in town that had become far too cramped as the children came into the world.

They had started walking home. It was late, now, almost six. Kerstin would probably be waiting impatiently with their meal, wondering why on earth they were so late.

The sky above them was winter black, the stars winking clear and bright. The snow out here was clean and white on the roofs and in the gardens. It was cold, ten degrees below. It was quiet, too, as the traffic sounds from the main road some way away could hardly be heard from where they were. The air was pure and clear, the snow lying on the bare bushes and trees like cotton wool. There was a heavy scent in the air, a calm scent of beauty and the depths of winter.

The little girl's eyes had shone and suddenly she was no longer tired.

"When we've eaten, I'm going out tobogganing," she had said.

"It's too late and too dark," he had said. "And we're going to decorate the tree tonight."

It suddenly struck him, three days before Christmas in the year 1977, that he'd forgotten to buy the tree.

He walked to Broad Street. He liked walking through the

town, not least at this time of year when the snow showed signs of being the kind of Christmas that was one of his most intensive childhood memories.

He looked up at August Hermansson's apartment, but it was dark, or rather there was no light in the window facing out onto Broad Street. He climbed the stairs and rang the bell. But the old man did not come to the door.

Holmberg wondered where he might be. Surely he hadn't left town?

He had a daughter in Molby and the idea had been that he should go there for Christmas, but Holmberg had told him not to go without telling him.

He was suddenly struck by a thought and began to walk toward the churchyard.

It was rather slippery and he heard a thump to his right, the snow rushing down the spire of All Saints Church. He passed the disused brewery, now threatened by the council's mania for demolition, with councillors of both parties this time in remarkable agreement. The hospital lay on his right, and on his left was the spacious churchyard.

Martin Holmberg knew few places as harmonious and melancholy as churchyards. The snow hung from the branches of the trees and had fallen like small woolly roofs onto the graves. He could hear the traffic in the distance, but here inside the gates it was like another world. Churchyards were always much more beautiful in winter when they were covered with snow.

He had once taken part in a discussion between two crime writers and policemen at the law society. Someone from the audience had told a story afterward about the churchyards in and around Edinburgh in the early nineteenth century.

A traveler had been amazed by the custom of relatives spending the night by their dear ones' graves in the light of lanterns. In all weathers, in the wet and cold, they kept up their vigil. The traveler had remarked on the beauty of the livings' reluctance to be parted from their dead.

His companion had shaken his head and laughed rather dryly.

It had had nothing to do with pleasant customs, the traveler had been informed. It was simply that families kept watch at nights, with gin as their only source of warmth, until the bodies had decayed. This was to scare off Burke and Hare and other body snatchers from coming to dig up the coffins and steal the corpses, which they then sold to

Dr. Robert Knox and others involved in anatomical studies at a time when medical science had a great need for corpses and had such trouble finding specimens.

He saw him in the distance.

August Hermansson was standing by his wife's grave, looking down at the wreaths still lying there since the burial five days before. The flowers and foliage had been somewhat damaged by the cold and the snow.

The tall gangling old man was looking almost transparent as he stood there, a kind of longing in his stance, his head bowed.

He was wearing a gray overcoat, a gray fur hat on his head and a gray scarf around his neck. He was standing in ankle-deep snow, immobile, as if pondering something profound.

Martin walked slowly over to him.

The old man turned his head without even raising his eyes.

"Good morning, Hermansson," said Martin quietly.

"Good morning, Holmberg."

They stood there in silence for a long while, side by side. The old man was the first to break the silence.

"It's so empty without her, but if she could speak, I know she would tell me that what happened was for the best."

"Yes."

"I couldn't have borne seeing her suffer."

"No."

"Maybe it's hard for someone else to understand. It was something between her and me. She asked me to do it. She didn't want to fade away. But that's probably hard for someone else to understand."

"No," said Holmberg. "I can understand that very well. So do we all. But the prosecutor has to take you to court. According to the law, it's murder. It's illegal to kill, even out of mercy."

"Would it have been more merciful to let her suffer?"

"I don't know. I mean, as a human being, I don't think so. But at the same time, I have to ask myself if one ever has the right to take another person's life."

"You're lying."

Martin started, unable to keep back a small smile.

"Does it show?"

"Yes," said the old man dryly.

"Yes, you're right. But I don't think I'd ever be able to bring myself to kill anyone, not even out of mercy."

August Hermansson nodded.

"No," he said. "It requires courage, I assure you. But perhaps one gets braver when one's older. In some ways, life seems no longer worth so much then. If the life you've had has been good. Please don't think I felt heroic when I did it. She was looking at me all the time, and smiling. And when I'd done it, she thanked me. Can you understand that? She thanked me. I wanted to scream at her to stop looking at me, stop smiling and keep quiet. But I couldn't. And when I stood there watching her die, I wanted to put an end to myself. But. . . my courage deserted me. I dared not. Can you understand that?"

"Yes."

"Strange. I'll never be able to understand that. So now I'll be tried, I suppose? Will I go to prison?"

"I don't know. But I don't think so."

"I see. So when will the trial be?"

"Not until in the new year. The prosecutor will tell us. I promise I'll let you know as soon as I know."

Hermansson looked up at the sky.

"I wish I'd had the courage to do away with myself, as well. What's the point of. . . what's the point of anything? She asked me to do it and I did it for love, and now I'm to be tried in court for something between her and me and God, if there is one. Will the court ever understand?"

"I think so. Humanly speaking, it's understandable, but from the point of view of the law . . . ."

"I know, I know. When will the laws be made to suit people?"

"It happens all the time. They're constantly being revised."

"In some fields, yes, but never the vital ones. Not in fields that affect us when we're dying."

"I'm sure there'll be a conditional sentence."

"What do I care about that? I refuse to let myself be tried for helping her."

Holmberg nodded. He understood. He understood so well. He didn't know what to say.

"Are you going anywhere over Christmas?" he said.

August Hermansson looked straight at him and in the depths of his eyes was a remote reflection, then a thin little smile appeared.

"Yes," he said. "I'm going away for Christmas."

"To your daughter's?"

Hermansson nodded.

"What's her address and telephone number?"

"I can't remember offhand. Can I phone you and tell you when I get back home?"

"Yes," said Holmberg. "I'll be at the police station until half-past four or five."

Hermansson nodded and Holmberg put out his hand.

Hermansson's handshake felt firm.

The old teacher looked him straight in the eye for a moment, then dropped his hand and without another word turned away and went on gazing at his wife's grave.

Holmberg felt stupid and superfluous. He nodded briefly and began walking slowly away. He tried to rid himself of his thoughts by thinking about what kind of wagons he would buy for his son's electric train, which already took up a large part of the floor of their basement.

MARTIN PUT THE CARRIER BAGS of Christmas parcels in his office and went into Olofsson's.

"I'm a bit late," he said.

"A bit? You've been out for about three and a half hours. Now you'd damned well better pull your socks up."

"There were so many people in the stores. Weren't we going to have a briefing on that terrorist?"

"We've done that. Do you think we can sit around waiting for you to honor us with your presence before we start?"

"Are you angry?"

Seved looked at the ceiling and flung out his arms.

"What do you think people would think if I went Christmas shopping in working hours?"

"I have, in fact, been talking to Hermansson, too."

"He phoned and wanted to speak to you. I promised you'd phone him when you got back. He said he would wait."

Martin sat down and scratched his head.

"The old man seems resigned. Sorrowful. Dispirited. It's a damned awful business, really."

"Tragic, I should say."

"And human."

"Aren't most cases that?"

"What?"

"Human?"

"Yes."

"Not this one," said Seved, holding out a photograph.

A face. A young man, hard to establish what age, but

probably between twenty-five and thirty. Black longish hair, piercing brown eyes, small round nose. Thin lips pressed together in a defiant line.

"That's the guy we've got to keep our eyes open for," said Seved.

"Oh, yes," sighed Holmberg.

"Security has been told by the West Germans that he's probably here in Sweden. They know he's been to Lund before, so it's presumed he might be here again now. Among other things, he had a girl here a year or two back. They've checked, but according to the girl, he hasn't been to see her yet. She doesn't know he might be back in town. Security has asked us to keep our eyes skinned, as I said. They've got people in shifts keeping watch outside the girl's place."

"Where does she live?"

"In one of the student residences. Dack House. The one on the corner of Chestnut Street and the South Esplanade."

"Are they keeping watch outside in a car all around the clock?"

"It wouldn't surprise me. Hope they've had the sense to use a civilian car. What they're demanding of us... no sorry, what they are *requesting* in the form of assistance from us is that we carry out a—and now I'm quoting them—'complementary reconnoitering element,' end of quote."

"To hold their hands, then, as simple as that?"

"Mainly, yes. If anyone sees him in town, he's to be arrested and taken to Security for interrogation."

"Oh, yes," said Martin, lighting a cigarette. "And of course the boy's probably changed his appearance by now, anyhow. They usually do, these terrorists. So he might well trot past them in the car without being recognized."

"We'll have to hope they've planted microphones in her room."

"Hmm. What's his name? It's quite useful to know a few practical details."

"His name's Herbert Ernfried Klein. The West Germans have discovered that he had something to do with the murder of Schleier."

"But he's not among those sixteen?"

"No, he's appeared like a joker during their searches and investigations. To add to it all, the Germans think he can explain some things about how the Baader lot got arms into their cells. In other words, it's quite an important spider in the web we've got to keep an eye out for."

"Why do they think he's here? Is there anything concrete to go on, or is it just that he's been to Lund before?"

"It's clear the Geramns have more than just an inkling, but whether they didn't want to say anything more to us, I don't know. Probably the former. So now all of us in the Crime Division as well as the Order Division have been given information and equipped with a photograph of the boy."

"Which is bound to be useless, as he couldn't be so dumb as not to change his appearance, could he?"

"I guess not," said Seved in agreement. "And should anyone happen to recognize him, it could be calculated that he's armed and wouldn't hesitate to shoot his way out. We know what happened in Holland."

"They shot the terrorists to pieces there." Martin Heaved a great sigh. "How much simpler it's been in dear little Lund, where our worst offenders are old men who commit mercy killings for love."

"Don't forget to phone him."

"You know, in some ways, I think it might be an interesting and useful trial."

"In what way?"

"The prosecution won't be able to shake Hermansson. He'll get a token sentence from a legal point of view, but he can't help winning a great moral victory, too. I'm sure of it."

"But mercy killings can't be made legal," protested Seved. "I mean, purely emotionally, yes. But—"

"They shoot horses, don't they? Just because they've broken a leg."

MARTIN HOLMBERG was back in his office, holding the color photograph of twenty-eight-year-old Herbert Ernfried Klein from Frankfurt.

He looked at it at arm's length, then went over to the filing cabinet on the left of the door and propped it up against a flowerpot containing a plastic tulip. Martin Holmberg was allergic to flowers, which gave him violent attacks of sneezing.

He sat down and gazed at the photograph.

The eyes...they fascinated him most, staring at him with a fanatical glow. He raised his right hand, pointing the forefinger as if he were holding a gun, and took sight along his arm.

"Bang!"

He picked up an eraser from his desk and threw it at the photograph, scoring a bull's-eye so that the photograph fell to the floor. The eraser bounced underneath the filing cabinet and he knew he would never get it out without moving the cabinet, and he would never be able to move that without emptying it of its contents.

He didn't want those eyes staring at him. They were so horribly alive...and at the same time dead, so full of a kind of death that made him uneasy.

His glance fell on the carrier bags full of Christmas presents.

Of course, yes.

He got up and went over to them. He tucked a long narrow parcel under his arm, went out into the corridor and across to Seved Olofsson's door. He opened it without knocking.

"I forgot this," he said.

"Have you bought me a Christmas present? Is it a sort of bribe because—"

"No, it's to Ragnar from us all."

"Ragnar?"

"Yes. You said he liked ice hockey so we thought, Kerstin and I, that a stick might come in useful."

Olofsson laughed, then shook his head and laughed even more loudly.

Holmberg looked at him in surprise.

"It's extraordinary," said Olofsson. "Ragnar had ice hockey on the brain last spring. This autumn we've had to take him into the rink in town three evenings a week for training. The day before yesterday, I thought he'd better have a new stick, so I went and bought him one for Christmas. That evening, Boel remembered to tell me she'd bought a stick for him three days earlier, and she was going to give it to him for Christmas. And now you."

Martin shrugged.

"Sorry," said Seved. "I shouldn't laugh when you've been so damned nice...but it does seem a bit comical, doesn't it?"

"Well, he can change it for something else...."

"Oh, he'll no doubt manage to break enough of them."

Martin nodded and left the room.

Olofsson stroked his beard, thinking about Ragnar.

Their adopted son was now seventeen.

He and Boel had at first been scared of taking the step of adopting him, scared of how he might turn out, scared of the responsibility, scared of what it all involved. They had been worried he might not accept them, worried he would never feel at home and a member of the family, and worried that they would overdo their care and love for him.

But it had turned out that they had never had to regret their decision and the boy really did seem to regard them as his parents.

Yes, thought Seved. He'll soon be going after girls and coming home drunk for the first time and needing help cleaning up after throwing up.

He wondered if Ragnar would be as concentrated in his interest in girls and going out on the spree as he was in all other things.

Ragnar had so much to catch up on, so much that he had never experienced. When he took an interest in something and began looking into it seriously, he did so with the most remarkable fervor, as if nothing else existed.

Just like ice hockey at this moment. Nothing else existed in his life except ice hockey. Before that it had been his moped, before that tennis.

The worst time had been when his passion for pop music had become straight sound-terrorism in the Olofsson home. But they had said nothing and suffered . . . and listened. They found it difficult, he and Boel, to begrudge him anything.

The door was flung open.

It was Martin.

"Did you say he said he would be at home waiting for me to phone?"

"Who?"

"Hermansson, of course," said Holmberg.

"Yes."

"I don't understand why he doesn't answer, then."

"Perhaps he's taking a leak or perhaps he's out."

"Not if he said he'd stay in."

"You don't think . . . ."

"I've a nasty feeling. . . ."

"I'll come with you."

He grabbed his jacket and hauled on his overcoat as he half ran along the corridor toward the elevator.

4

THE OTHER MAN

WERNER SODERSTROM went through the door of the police station feeling lost and uncertain. It was the first time he had ever been there.

He was directed from reception up to the second floor and finally found a door with the name Stefan Elg on it.

He knocked.

"Come in."

A man with ash-blond hair was sitting at a desk, looking toward the door.

"Good morning," said Soderstrom. "I was told to come here. It's about a missing person."

"Do you wish to report a missing person?"

"Yes, a person has disappeared. I think. Or rather, we do."

The fair man frowned. "You think? Who is missing?"

"That's what we don't know."

Stefan Elg closed his eyes and shook his head.

"Say that again, would you?"

"Well, it's rather a long story."

"But the content is that you don't know if someone's disappeared, and if someone has disappeared, you don't know who has, is that it?"

"Just about."

"That's about the oddest thing I've ever heard. Sit down and tell me."

"Well, where shall I begin?"

"From the beginning."

He gave a verbose, complicated and thorough account. Several times Elg seemed to be about to interrupt to ask something, but each time Soderstrom's voice hesitated as if about to stop and let the policeman speak, the inspector waved his hand and shook his head.

Then Soderstrom came to Thursday the fifteenth. The end, in fact.

Elg peered at him through the thick cloud of cigarette smoke. He took a long drag, leaned forward and stubbed his cigarette out in the ashtray. Then he leaned back again and sucked in his lips.

"This is extremely interesting," he said. "And I'm not being ironic. This man has been appearing for five years, if I've got it right, and now he's suddenly disappeared."

Soderstrom nodded.

"But it could have been longer, too?"

"Well," said Soderstrom, "I don't think so. Because Gerd started talking about him in '72, and if he'd been going on his nightly walks before that, I'm sure she would have noticed him and told us all."

"Gerd?"

"An elderly woman who lived two floors below us. She died last year."

"It's quite amazing," said Elg, smiling broadly. "He came along there, night after night, and just stood there on the corner and stared. Then turned on his heel and walked back. Quite fantastic. But tell me something. Surely you didn't keep a lookout every evening?"

Soderstrom grimaced.

"No," he said. "We didn't look every night to see if he was coming."

"So he might quite well have gone away weeks before without you noticing it?"

"It's. . .that's possible."

"How often did you look out?"

"Hard to say. . .now and again. But there was always someone in the building looking. He became a kind of subject of conversation for us all. The time he was away, it got around like lightning. At least two people had looked out and noticed that he hadn't come, and they told the others, and it wasn't long before everyone had been informed he was missing. If he'd been missing several times and for longer periods, I'm sure someone would have noticed, and the news would have spread very quickly."

"I see."

Elg picked up a yellow pencil and rolled it between his palms. "What do you want us to do?"

"I thought. . .I thought that if something had happened. . . ."

"I understand. But you must see we can do very little. A totally unknown person stops following a long-established routine. We can't just start investigating a person who as far as anyone knows has done nothing.''

"It's not so much that he might have done something, but that something might have happened to him.''

"Yes. He may have grown tired of his nightly walks. He may have moved out of town. He may be ill at home. He may have gone away for Christmas.''

"So you're not going to try to find out whether anything has happened to him?''

"As I told you, and I really meant it, the mystery of it may catch one's imagination, but on the other hand there could be a huge number of natural explanations. We can't just start an investigation on such a weak basis.''

"I see.''

"But I'm very grateful you came and told me all this. If it should so happen . . . if we hear of anything that might be connected with what you've told me, then we know. But as it is now . . . .'' Elg shook his head.

"Oh,'' said Soderstrom, his disappointment evident in his voice. "Well, then, all I can say is thank you.''

"I'm the one who should be thanking you,'' said Elg. "And if he pops up again, then everything'll be all right.''

"Yes,'' said Soderstrom. "But I can't shake off the feeling that something might have happened. It's not just me, either. Lots of the others are convinced there's something odd about his sudden disappearance.''

Elg nodded.

"But if you're so curious about him, why didn't you ever follow him? To find out who he was and where he came from.''

"Well, it didn't work out like that. . . .''

Elg smiled.

When Soderstrom left the police station, it was with a feeling of not having been taken seriously.

But Elg was left sitting sunk in his thoughts. Then he got up and went across to the window. He looked down onto the yard where the snow was already in thick drifts. He leaned his forehead against the glass and thought.

He thought of his grandfather, who had been a hundred and two years old when he died. He'd been a farmer in the Vimmerby area. Stefan had spent a lot of time on the farm when he was a child and later as a youth.

Stefan had always wondered about one thing.

Every evening after their evening meal his grandfather

had got up from the table with a contented sigh and a quiet thank-you, and then without saying anything he had put his cap on and gone out. Exactly fifty-five minutes later he would be back, punctually as if timed.

His grandfather didn't have a wristwatch, but he had a sturdy turnip watch that he kept in his waistcoat pocket on Saturdays and Sundays and all public holidays. On the other days, it hung on a nail above his bed. But even on weekday evenings when he went out for his fifty-five minutes he always came back punctually, as if some inbuilt mechanism measured the time for him.

As a child Stefan hadn't thought all that much about his grandfather's walks. When very young he had once asked where the old man was going, but his grandfather hadn't replied. He had only turned around and looked at him with a smile and an expression in his eyes as if he hadn't understood the question. When Stefan had asked his grandmother, she had simply replied, "Out."

Then when he was adolescent, he had once asked his grandfather if he could come with him, but the old man had just shaken his head.

"Where does he go?" Stefan asked.

"He goes for his evening walk," they had told him.

The next evening Stefan had followed him.

He had seen his grandfather disappearing into the forest along a path and then up to a bare smooth rock. The old man had stopped there and then stood quite still, just stood there, looking.

The third time Stefan had followed him his grandfather had seen him. After standing there for twenty minutes, he had turned around and spotted Stefan as he had started walking back again.

It was the first time Stefan had ever seen his grandfather really angry.

"What are you doing here?" he had said roughly.

"I only . . . only wanted to know where you went."

"Can't a man even take his evening walk in peace now?"

"I didn't mean anything. . . ."

"No, no. But a man likes to be on his own sometimes."

"But you're always out for exactly the same length of time. Do you always come here?"

His grandfather sat down on a felled pine and looked at the smooth rock.

"Yes," he said. "You're quite right. I've come here every

single evening for almost fifty years now. I'd never thought about it before."

Stefan had sat down beside him.

"But why just here?"

His grandfather had looked around at the forest, the trees, the grass, the stones, the bushes, the leaves and the flowers.

"I don't know," he said. "It just happened like that. When you've worked all day . . . it's calm and peaceful here, so quiet. Come."

So he had gone ahead up onto the bare smooth rock.

"Look around," he said.

Stefan had glimpsed the lake through the trees and seen the rolling countryside on the other side of the lake. He had heard the branches and leaves rustling in the evening breeze. He had heard the birds as if through a filter. He had smelled the scents of the forest. He had breathed them in deeply and was intoxicated by a strange contentment.

He had understood, but he would never be able to articulate what he had understood.

The following year his grandfather had sold the farm and moved to an apartment in Vimmerby.

His grandfather had stopped his evening walks. He suddenly seemed to age, becoming ancient and crumpled. But he had lived until he was a hundred and two, a tiny, brittle old man just before he died, quite white haired and thin on top, his face wrinkled, his hands trembling.

"You know what?" he had said to Stefan the last time they met. "Do you know what I've missed most all these years here in town? I'll tell you. The forest. I've missed my evening walks. I haven't been a human being since I lost them. Here in town there's nowhere to go for the same thing. You know what? I'd very much like to go just once again into the forest and smell the smell of moss, of leaves and resin and cleanliness."

A week later his grandfather had died.

Stefan lighted a cigarette and went to see Frits Sture, the commissioner, who ought to know about this business, in spite of everything.

As he walked along the corridor toward the commissioner's office, he thought, a change happened in his life, of course.

Sture held the same view.

"Yes," he said. "It's a good thing we know about it,

should something crop up, but we can't waste time investigating anything so vague. Hell, he may simply have moved away. Or fallen in love. Perhaps he's married, so he hasn't got the time for evening walks any longer.''

"Or perhaps he was already married," said Stefan. "And then they had children...and we all know what that means. Kids have to be fed at that time, and diapers changed. Everything changes when you've got little kids."

"Hmm," grunted Sture, who had no children, so he didn't know. "By the way, could he give a description of him at all?"

"No," said Elg. "No one seems to have seen him properly. But he seems to have had a beard."

"Well, that's something. But then his appearance probably has nothing to do with it. I don't think we can do anything about it all. How's the Gota bank robbery going? Have you got anywhere with that yet?"

"Yes. Both of them have admitted it, but that third man said to be with them...according to them, anyhow doesn't seem to exist. At any rate, not at the address they gave."

"A remarkable story. But it'll soon be Christmas now. Then we can relax for a couple of days. That'll be good."

5

THE MAN

IT WAS TEN TO SEVEN by the time Martin Holmberg got home.
Anders was in his pajamas, just off to bed. The twins, Maria
and Magdalena, were having a pillow fight on their parents'
bed, and big sister Inger was trying to quiet them so that she
could hear the radio without having it blaring. Kerstin was
mopping up the bathroom floor, as Anders's bath had been
a lively watery battle.

"Hello!" Martin called as soon as he got through the door.

The sound of the twins hurtling down the stairs was like a
stampede of wild horses.

"Daddy's been buying Christmas presents!" they
chorused. "What've you bought?"

"You'll see when the time comes. Have you been good today?"

"Oh, yes," said Maria.

"Mommy hasn't been cross with us all day," said Magdalena.

"Only a little," said Maria.

"Only when we put snow through the mail slot," said
Magdalena.

"You see?" said Kerstin from the top of the stairs, a floor
cloth in one hand and Anders under her other arm.

"Daddy!" he crowed, stretching out his arms.

"Hello, old man. How's things?"

"You're late," said Kerstin.

"Yes, it's been that kind of day."

"There's a meat loaf in the oven. It's probably still hot."

"Hello," said Inger, looking sulky as she slipped down the
stairs and went on past him into the living room to turn on
the television.

Maria and Magdalena rushed after her.

"Scram out of here!" cried Inger. "I want to watch."

"So do we, so do we!"

"It's not for kids. Anyhow, you should go to bed now."

"No, we shouldn't!"

"Daddy!" crowed Anders, literally throwing herself out of Kerstin's arms across to Martin, who caught him, then kissed Kerstin.

"Anything special today?" she said.

"Tell you later. How've things been for you?"

"They're lively, as usual. Stop bothering Inger now!" she called into the living room. "Maria and Magdalena! Upstairs now and get undressed. Time for bed."

"No, we want to stay up late tonight," said Maria.

"As late as Inger!" said Magdalena. "We want to watch TV."

Anders clambered down and ran in to sit down in front of the television set.

It was half-past eight before Anders was asleep, the twins in bed and Inger had cleaned her teeth before getting into bed for a short read.

"We had a Christmas card from the Malmgrens today," said Kerstin, while Martin was eating. "Did we send them one?"

"I don't know. You addressed them all. But if they were on the list, I expect we did."

"There's one from Seved and Boel, too."

"It's silly sending cards when we see each other every day and live so near to each other. Hermansson committed suicide."

Kerstin looked startled. "What?"

"The old man who helped his wife."

"Oh, God."

"He put the plug in the basin, filled it with water and cut his arteries." Martin shook his head. "It's so meaningless. When we're old, and if one of us gets—well, incurable cancer, for instance, could you imagine killing me if I asked you to?"

She bit her bottom lip, rummaging through the heap of Christmas cards.

"*I* would want *you* to, if I asked you to, at any rate," she said quietly.

"That's no answer to my question."

"I don't know if I'd dare."

"Neither do I. But suffering is hard to bear for the person who has to watch it, too."

"Yes. There's a letter for you over by the radio, by the way. I almost forgot."

It was an ordinary white envelope, postmarked Lund. He opened it by tearing off one corner and using his little finger as a paper knife. It contained a white card. The sender had pasted a picture of a Christmas gnome on it, but a death's-head had been stuck over the gnome's face.

He turned it over.

The back was blank.

"Who's it from?"

"Some joker or other, I suppose. Damned silly joke. But things like that happen. What were you going to do this evening?"

"Make toffee and fudge."

He got up, crumpled up the death's-head gnome and threw card and envelope into the bin under the sink. Then he cleared the table.

"I'm just going to take a shower. Could you put the coffee on, then we can have it before you start on the toffee making? Seved sends his love, by the way, and thanks us for the hockey stick for Ragnar. He's got three for Christmas!"

"What did you buy today? I thought we'd bought enough for the children."

"I saw a few things in the toy department . . . and there's something for you."

"What?" she said, getting up.

"You're as nosy as the kids. Not until Santa comes."

"I don't believe in Santa."

"Disgraceful. And all the trouble I take to look like him! I've even bought a new beard."

He put his arm around her waist and pulled her to him, running a finger down her spine and whispering in her ear.

"No," she said. "You can take a shower by yourself. But do it now, because I don't want to have to make the toffee on my own."

The telephone rang.

Martin lifted the receiver.

Silence.

"Hello," he said.

Then he heard a click as when a receiver is replaced, and a few seconds later the dial tone sounded again.

He shrugged his shoulders and banged the receiver down.

"Wrong number," he said as he climbed the stairs.

He had a hot shower, and it seemed as if all his fatigue was been rinsed away. As he dried himself he realized how much he was looking forward to Christmas and not having to think about work until after New Year's.

By the time he had dressed, he had got rid of his depressing thoughts about August Hermansson. And forgotten the card with the death's-head gnome. And the telephone call that wasn't a telephone call.

He was in a really good mood as he went downstairs to help Kerstin make toffee.

THE OTHER MAN

WERNER SODERSTROM had gone reluctantly to the police, although he had thought it necessary and sensible. But he had left the station with a feeling of dissatisfaction and failure, as well as with some disappointment. Now he was feeling inspired by a conviction that he was a chosen person.

All in all, four people had looked out of their windows facing the street that evening. Two of them had turned back into the room and exclaimed, "Come and look. He's back again!"

But they had been answered with, "That's Werner! Can't you see?"

"What use would that be? What can you achieve by doing that?" Lisa had said, when he had explained that he could not rest until he found out something about this unknown man.

"I don't know."

Now he was standing on the corner of Maria Street and Merchant Street. It was a sharp, clear, still night, the cold crackling in the branches and the silence uncanny.

This was where he used to stand.

What had he been looking at?

Werner could see apartment blocks, he could see along Merchant Street as far as the crossroads with Town Hall Street, the corner of the Domus Store over there on Town Hall Street. He could see the Methodist Church, apartment blocks, a stretch of Maria Street straight ahead, sloping slightly uphill. He could see the Mission Church and apartment blocks. A cyclist. He could see parked cars. To the right he could see along Merchant Street as far as where the street became a steep hill down to the pond. He could see the brow of the hill, but not over it. More apartment blocks. Behind him he had the brewery fence and an office block.

What had he been looking at?

Werner looked up at the apartment windows.

How many people had seen him here? How many people had missed him? How many had wondered who he was and what he did, what he was doing there and what he was staring at?

He caught a glimpse of a face behind a curtain, the curtain moving. Then the room turned dark. His glance wandered from window to window.

To whom could he go to find out who the unknown man was? Might any of the people here have gone down and exchanged a few words with him? Asked him why he was standing there? Perhaps even been given an explanation?

Someone who had driven him away?

Had the unknown man an acquaintance who lived here? Whom he was keeping an eye on? But why, in that case, only for that relatively short time each night?

Had he seen something one evening and then returned night after night to . . . well, to what?

But this was where he had stood.

The cold was stinging Werner's cheeks, and his toes were numb, his fingers stiff. A shudder ran right through him.

He turned around and looked down the length of Maria Street.

That was where he had come from.

He looked at his watch. Eight minutes past ten.

What on earth did he think he could achieve by standing here? As if the answer to the question were here. By walking in the same direction as he had . . . from where he had come, to where he had gone. There, somewhere, in that direction, was the answer. But where?

He began to walk.

He walked relatively slowly, trying to remember the manner in which the other man had walked.

He walked past his own apartment house and looked up at the lighted windows.

Lisa was standing in the window. He waved to her, but she did not wave back.

No doubt she thinks I'm behaving like a fool.

He went on, past the People's Hall.

He had the park on his left now, the apartment houses on the other side of the road on his right.

He walked at a slow pace, and as he walked he looked at the apartment houses on his right.

How many people living along the street had seen him and started looking out now and again to see if he was there as usual? How many were now wondering why he wasn't coming by as usual? First northward . . . and then back again.

Did the unknown man live in one of those apartment blocks?

"Good evening. Haven't seen you for a few evenings."

He turned around.

Someone was walking toward him along one of the park paths, a dog on a lead behind him.

"Good evening," said Werner guardedly.

"Oh, I beg your pardon," the other man said. 'I thought you were someone I knew."

Werner nodded, then went on, but after ten steps or so he stopped and turned around.

The man who had said good evening to him was crossing the street. The dog on the lead was a dachshund.

Werner found it hard to decide, but then the man turned around and looked at him, and that made up his mind for him. He had to try, at least.

He crossed the road.

"Excuse me," said Werner. "My name's Soderstrom, Werner Soderstrom. I live a little farther up the street."

"Yes?" said the other man, looking at him. "My name's Svensen," he added, after hesitating for a moment over the conventions that politeness demanded once he had realized that Soderstrom wished him no harm.

"You see," said Werner, "it may sound rather strange to you, but I wonder if. . . . You mistook me for someone else— who did you think I was?"

"Sorry?"

"You mistook me for someone else. Who did you think I was?"

"Only another person. What do you mean?"

"Well, it may sound rather peculiar, but I am trying to find out who a certain person might be and whether anything has happened to him."

"Oh, yes?" said Svensen, with some interest.

"It's like this. . .for several years, someone has been walking past our window onto the corner of Merchant Street, and then standing there for a while, just looking at nothing. He hasn't been there for several nights, and I feel something might have happened to him, as he's stopped coming."

He looked down at the dachshund sniffing at his shoe.

"Yes," said Svensen. "The fact is that for several years I've stopped for a few words with a person who used to take a walk along here. What does the person you're looking for look like?"

"I don't really know. I never really saw him properly, only from the window. But he's a bit bowed and a little—well, how can I put it—he sort of lopes along. And then he's got a beard."

"Yes, that must be him."

Werner leaned down and patted the dachshund, which at once leaped back to its master.

"All right, Ture, calm down," said Svensen. "It's almost a week since I last saw him."

"Do you know him?"

"No, I haven't the slightest idea who he is. What makes you think something's happened to him?"

"It's hard to explain. It's mostly just a feeling. I mean, why should he stop coming, if nothing's happened?"

"Yes, that's a thought. But on the other hand, it needn't be something unpleasant, need it?"

"No, of course not. There could be lots of ordinary explanations. The police gave me some today."

"The police? Have you been to the police?"

"Yes."

"About his not coming anymore?"

"Yes."

"Good gracious. You *have* become involved!"

"Yes," said Werner, laughing. "It seems so."

"I don't know anything about him. We used to chat for a moment, that's all. That started years ago. We moved here, my wife and I, in '69. We got Ture in '71. The dog, I mean."

Werner nodded and looked down at the dachshund, which was now trying to hide behind Svensen's legs.

Svensen was a man of about his own age, in his fifties. He had a bushy mustache and a beaky nose, the rest of his head covered by a fur hat and scarf and earmuffs. He was tall, but it was hard to see whether he was powerfully built or slim, because his overcoat looked very thick. He was wearing strong boots on his feet.

"I've always taken the dog out at night, and I usually do so at exactly the same time. It was as if he had a time fuse inside him, the rascal. We started nodding to each other after a couple of years. There aren't many people about these days, but this man came along every single night. So after a while we started nodding to each other. Rather like people do morning after morning on the bus or the train. You feel you almost know them in the end."

"When did you start coming across him?"

"Let me think. The summer? No, probably in the autumn, four or five years ago. It must have been '72, I think. Yes, that's it. Seventy-two."

"Did you talk to him then?"

"Yes. The nodding went on for quite a while. Then we started saying good evening when we met, but nothing else until one evening he suddenly stopped and spoke to me. But that was much later, the following spring. Seventy-three, it must have been. 'Spring in the air,' he said, or something like that. I didn't think so, because it was really quite cold. But I agreed with him. One doesn't like to be rude. So then we started exchanging the odd word or having a chat every night."

Werner Soderstrom thought for a moment.

"May I ask what you talked about? I mean, didn't he ever say what he was up to out at that time of night?"

"No," said Svensen, slightly surprised. "No, he didn't. I didn't think much about it. What did we talk about? You may well ask. Nothing special, anyhow. The weather and topical things and things that'd happened."

"Nothing that would help us to find out who he was or what he did?"

"No. It's really rather silly, I suppose. I mean, here I am without the slightest clue about a person I've chatted with for nights on end. It's ridiculous, really. We just chatted for a few moments—about nothing, mostly. About vandals, the election, atomic energy, hijackings and terrorism, schools and young people today . . . you know, everything you can think of. It became quite a pleasant habit, chatting with the man."

Soderstrom nodded.

"It's just struck me . . . did you ever see his fingers? Or his hands?"

"What would be special about them?"

"I just thought . . . perhaps he was wearing a wedding ring?"

Svensen frowned and lifted up the whining dog. It had long been trying to interrupt the conversation and persuade its master to go indoors into the warmth.

"I don't remember, if I ever noticed."

"What did he look like?"

"Look like? What a question...I'm hopeless at describing people. Apart from his beard, of course. He looked like most people. He certainly hadn't anything special about him. But he smoked those cigarillos, by the way. He offered me one one evening, but as I don't smoke, I refused it. Terrible if something's happened to him. Such a pleasant man. What are the police doing about it?"

"Nothing."

"Nothing?"

"No. The man I spoke to said the police couldn't start looking for him on such vague evidence. They didn't even know if he really had disappeared. And he hadn't done anything, had he?"

"Do people have to come to harm before the police take an interest?"

"We don't know if he has come to any harm."

"No, but his disappearance does seem peculiar. You've made me quite interested, I must say."

"He never said where he lived, did he?"

"No," said Svensen. "He went on in that direction, but I don't know where he went."

The street went uphill for a stretch before running downhill again.

"Once I happened to turn around just as he went on over the hill and then vanished out of sight. I can see it now, him walking on, then vanishing into the mist."

Werner looked up the hill and sighed. Then he took off his glove and scratched his cheek.

"Are you going to go on?" said Svensen.

"No, I think I'll give up for this evening. I've made a little progress, anyhow."

"I was just thinking. . . will you be coming tomorrow?"

"Yes, I think so. I don't think I'll be happy until I've sorted this out."

"Couldn't we do it together?"

"I've nothing against it."

"You've made me curious now. Are you working tomorrow during the day?"

"No, we're on holiday over Christmas and New Year's."

"Then perhaps we could meet sometime tomorrow and go on?"

"Yes, certainly. What time?"

"Shall we do it during the day, or wait until the evening?"

"I don't know. We could try daytime."

"All right, let's. What about meeting here at. . .does midday suit you?"

"Yes, fine."

"Then let's say midday. My name's Alec, by the way. It'll be easier if we use first names, won't it?"

"Yes, indeed. My name's Werner."

"Yes, so you said. Well, see you tomorrow, then."

"Yes. Goodbye for now."

Werner walked back home.

He was looking forward to the next day with considerable curiosity and expectation.

He wondered what Lisa would say when he got back.

When all was said and done, she was the one who had been most curious about the unknown man in the first place.

Werner felt he had come one step closer.

Just one step.

7

THE MAN

THEY HAD GONE TO BED in the small hours of the morning. It was all of half-past one by the time the toffee and fudge had been finished, the mulled wine made and tasted, and the Christmas preparations sufficiently advanced that they considered they could go to bed. Even then, they hadn't fallen asleep until almost quarter-past two.

It was quite dark when Martin woke. He was at once wide-awake and knew immediately what had woken him.

He managed to extract his arm without waking Kerstin, then hurried out to answer the persistently ringing telephone before it woke the children.

The floor was cold, the whole house cold. He almost fell over a heap of building bricks on the top landing, but he managed to grab at the banister rail.

He listened for sounds from the children's rooms, but the echoing thump of falling bricks had not disturbed them, though the telephone was still ringing at full volume.

He hurried on downstairs and snatched up the receiver.

"Hello," he said.

No one answered.

He frowned, noticing he was shaking with cold.

"Hello. Is anyone there? Hello."

No reply.

There was a click. Then a few moments later the dial tone. He stood still, the receiver in his hand, the dial tone singing in his ear.

He put the receiver down, turned the phone over and set the volume at lowest.

Then he went slowly up the stairs and crept back into bed, pulling the covers closely around him. He was cold. He moved closer to Kerstin, who twitched in her sleep and retreated slightly from the chill of his body.

He curled up, feeling wide-awake.

Two minutes later, he was asleep.

He woke up at a quarter to eight and could hardly open his eyes.

He stretched out his hand toward Kerstin, but he was alone in the bed. He blinked at the light out on the landing and yawned.

His whole body felt weary.

What had he done last night? He vaguely remembered getting up in the middle of the night. But what the hell had he done?

Kerstin came in carrying Anders, his feed bottle in her hand.

"Good morning," she said.

"Morning."

"You do look sleepy. Here you are, this'll wake you up."

She held the boy out and Martin took his yelling son, whose eager fingers were grabbing for the bottle. He drew aside the cover, put his son alongside him and tucked them both in. Then he put the child's head on the pillow and pushed the teat into his mouth. With a loud slurp and triumphant squeal Anders began sucking at it.

Kerstin crept down into the warmth of her side of the bed.

"Did you wake in the night?" he said.

"Wake? No. Why?"

"You don't know if I got up or not?"

"Did you get up in the night?"

"I don't know. I have a faint idea the phone rang and I got up to answer it. But I've no definite memory of it."

She shook her head doubtfully.

"If the phone had rung, one of the kids or I would have woken. You must've dreamed it."

"I suppose so."

"Who did you dream you were talking to?"

"Don't know. I've an idea someone hung up on me."

"What about yesterday evening?" she said.

"What?"

"Don't you remember? The phone went and no one spoke when you answered."

"Of course, that wrong number."

"You must have dreamed about that."

"Yes. Yes, that was it, I expect. Surely... if I'd got up in the night, I'd remember it."

When he came down for breakfast, he looked over at the telephone. He lifted the receiver and heard the dial tone.

He turned the phone over and saw the volume control was on the minimum. He grimaced, shrugged and put the phone down.

There was something he ought to remember, but he couldn't.

"Damned silly you can never really remember what you've dreamed," he said.

"Do you have to make such a row at night?" said Inger.

"What do you mean?"

"Someone was blundering about last night."

"Blundering?"

"Yes, a sort of rattling thumping."

"When?"

"I don't know."

"Did you hear the phone ring last night?"

"No. But you were laughing and making an awful lot of noise before you went to bed. Later on, too. You were making an awful row in your room. What were you doing?"

"Uhum," said Martin "I expect the mulled wine was a bit strong."

He emptied his glass of juice with a grimace.

HE DROVE AROUND via South Esplanade on his way to the police station, stopping just before the crossroads by Raby Street to look at Dack House, a nine-story block of student apartments. He lighted a cigarette and wondered whether the Security people were in some other car somewhere around, keeping watch on the block.

There would be a fuss if Security caught their terrorist in that apartment house, which was owned by Smaland province and was for Smaland students. They were known to be the most extreme lefties in Lund, a hotbed of radicals and loudmouthed idealists who were unable to see reality for their revolutionary dreams.

He accelerated slightly and the car moved off. A blue bus lumbered past, emitting clouds of fumes. It braked jerkily and lurched into the bus stop just ahead of him.

Then he saw the car on the left-hand side of the esplanade. A white Amazon. Two men were in the front, trying to look as if they weren't there. He presumed that wasn't the only car, as Herbert Klein was considered such a hot potato.

He himself regarded everything to do with terrorists and terrorism with loathing, hatred and also a hefty dose of fear. While he was opposed to capital punishment, he felt that the death sentence could be justified emotionally as a desperate reaction to terrorism. Humanly and intellectually, though, it was unacceptable.

But he knew that he himself would act as executioner if someone close to him were struck by terrorists. Then he would not hesitate to take revenge, an eye for an eye, a tooth for a tooth. He would find it hard to endure the thought of society stepping in between as a kind of acting executioner. If such a situation should arise, he would want to be the person holding the ax.

He didn't think such a situation would ever arise. But a thought occasionally persisted at the back of his mind that it wasn't just policemen who took risks; that their families were also in the line of fire. That was the dirtiest of all the rules of the game, and made policemen very vulnerable. But that was hardly of concern in Sweden. As yet.

He was almost certain the hunt for Klein would remain a Security Police matter and that the Lund police would not be involved. They would just give the routine cooperation to their colleagues from Security. The whole thing would probably fizzle out, anyhow.

It was ten past nine when he went through the door of the police station in Lund on December 23, 1977.

OLOFSSON BROUGHT THE NEWS.

"Hello," he said, testing out the scene. "How are you feeling today?"

"Fine," said Holmberg. "Why?"

"Well, a little matter has arisen . . . or rather, there's a slight mess-up, to say the least of it . . . and, um, I need your help a bit."

Holmberg pushed the typing desk away and turned slowly around in his chair.

"It's Christmas Eve tomorrow," said Olofsson.

"Had you possibly thought that I didn't know that?"

"Oh, yes, naturally you know that."

"Okay, what the hell are you getting at?"

"Well, you're on compensatory leave over Christmas and the New Year, aren't you?"

"Yes."

Holmberg was beginning to have a faint idea what was coming and slowly got to his feet.

He looked at Olofsson. Then he slowly shook his head and held both hands up, palms forward, and smiled nastily.

"Oh, no. You can't try that one. I know. The holiday roster is in a mess and now you're wondering whether I might possibly be so splendidly kind enough to help you out a bit in making up the duty list so that the town will not be without policemen over Christmas and the New Year. Fifteen men have got influenza, seventeen have broken their legs and all the others have got leprosy. You've worked it out that I am the only perfectly fit one left at the moment who is also in town over the holiday. And with the thought that I'll be spending Christmas in Lund anyhow, you were wondering whether I would possibly not like to do that in this beloved police station. My family? But, my dears, I'd be delighted to bring my wife and kids here, and then we could all dance around the Christmas tree with the drunks and crooks over the holiday. Nothing should affect the family's Christmas. Oh, no. And naturally I would be able to take compensatory leave as soon as the holiday is over, and then I can have twice as long leave and you've already fixed it that I shall be going to the Canary Islands then, and you've suggested I should be awarded some kind of travel grant for it and—"

"Have you finished?" said Olofsson, looking uncomfortable. "I wasn't actually going to ask you to work."

"No?"

"Well, not here, I mean."

"Oh, no?"

"No."

"Where, then?"

"Things have gone wrong. Wilke, Berg and Stillgren were to have been on standby duty over Christmas. This is only over the actual Christmas days."

"Don't tell me all three of them have got sick simultaneously? That would be too much of a good thing."

"Stillgren is off sick. High temperature and severe cough. Wilke has broken his leg and will be in a cast for a month. Berg's mother died yesterday. And—"

"Yes?"

"So it's standby duty in question. You know, at home, but prepared for anything the ordinary duty man can't manage. It wouldn't be much. . . I mean, the risk of being called out is minimal."

"Oh, yes. So I'm to go instead of all three of them?"

"No, not alone."

"Who else have you managed to persuade?"

"Leif. And I thought I'd be the third."

Holmberg looked out of the window and pursed his mouth. "But what if something happens? That means I can't be at home for a single bloody minute over the whole of Christmas. Kerstin would strangle me and the children will refuse to know me."

"If anything should happen, then you'd be called out under any circumstances."

"Okay, then, for Christ's sake, before you start appealing to the patriotic feelings I haven't got."

"Thanks. I knew I could count on you."

"Did you?"

"Yes."

"That's what's wrong. We know each other far too well."

"Buddy!" said Olofsson, smiling and thumping Martin on the back. "That's right, Boel told me to ask you if you and Kerstin and the children would like to look in on us on Boxing Day and have a bite to eat. If you hadn't planned anything else, that is, of course."

"Give my love to Madame Olofsson and say we would be delighted."

"Certainly."

"But we won't be able to drink."

"What?"

"If we're on standby duty. Supposing we have to go out? It would look nice if we'd just had one over the eight, wouldn't it?"

"Oh, we'll risk that."

"Buddy!"

Olofsson smiled and Holmberg started laughing.

"Anything new on the terrorist?"

"No," said Olofsson. "A couple of guys came in to get warm this morning. The ones who'd been outside the house all night. They were complaining it was cold and boring staring at student apartments all night."

"Are they keeping people there all over Christmas, too?"

"Yes, I think so."

Holmberg laughed. "Bet you they'll have a Christmas tree with a Swedish flag on top in the back of the car," he said. "Out with you, now, so I can get my reports done. I've got a damned great pile of paperwork to do before I can go on Christmas leave."

"Christmas leave?"

Holmberg hurled a large eraser at the escaping Olofsson, who just managed to retreat in time. The eraser bounced against the door and up into the air, straight at the flowerpot on the filing cabinet. The pot tipped over and fell to the floor.

"Hell!" he said, starting to pick up the fragments.

When he saw the earth on the floor, it struck him as really rather idiotic having a plastic tulip in a flowerpot full of earth.

8

THE OTHER MAN

ALEC SVENSEN was waiting in the cold when Werner arrived, as well wrapped up as on the day before.

"Hello," said Werner. "Well, we're off. No dachshund?"

"No, I've left him at home. My wife thinks I'm nuts."

"So does mine, really, but she's just as curious as I am."

They started walking.

"So you're married, too, are you?" said Alec.

"Yes. What do you do? I mean, for your living?"

"Sell tickets on the railways."

"Do you, now?"

"And you?"

"I work at Bergwall's Hardware Store."

"And you can take time off at this time of the year? I'd have thought you'd be very busy?"

"Some people have to shop, too."

He laughed.

"Oh, well," he said. "What now?"

"Yes, that's the question. I've been thinking. What about calling on people living along the street and asking if any of them have seen him?"

"We might do that. You mean at random, just like that? We couldn't ask all of them. We'd never get through the whole street by Easter."

"No, just a few. They won't all be at home, will they?"

"I wondered whether we could try the people in the apartment houses all around the corner of Maria Street and Merchant Street? You know, where he used to stand."

"But that wouldn't get us any nearer to him, would it?"

"No, but someone there might know him."

"Best would be if we could find out where he lives. He must live somewhere around here, otherwise he wouldn't have chosen just this street for his walks."

"Unless something special drew him here."

"There's that, of course. But don't you think we should try this out first?"

"Yes, perhaps we should."

The snow crunched under their feet and the cold stung their cheeks.

Two hours later they had got to where Maria Street, Bridge Street, Park Street and Soran Street all met, by the police station and its neighboring fire station.

There were three of them by then.

They had called at twenty-three apartments. Fifteen had opened their doors. Twelve of the people who had come to the door had been willing to talk, once the two men had explained their mission. The thirteenth muttered something about not being interested. The fourteenth threatened to call the police if they didn't go away. The fifteenth, a woman, was interested enough to join them.

Of the remaining twelve, none knew whom they were talking about. Seven said they weren't in the slightest bit interested in who used to walk past and had now disappeared. Of the remaining two, one, a woman of about thirty, said she'd always thought there was something frightening about the man, and she'd been scared whenever she'd seen him. She thought it was wonderful that he'd disappeared, as now she wouldn't have to think there was anything horrid about him.

The second person declared an interest in the gentleman and said it was quite empty now that he'd gone. But who he was, she had no idea. A pity in some ways that he had disappeared, because somehow he'd been part of the scene.

The woman who had joined them was called Barbara Johansson. She was thirty-nine and worked part-time. She was married to a free-lance mechanic who was coming home on Christmas Eve.

She had short bobbed hair and was tall and slim.

She had joined them because she had become inexplicably intrigued by the unknown stroller, and now that he had disappeared she wanted to know what had become of him.

"He's always intrigued me," she explained. "It was pure chance I happened to notice him a few years back...three years ago, I think. I looked out of the window and there he was. Nothing special about that. I mean, there are lots of people out walking at night. But then I got it into my head he would appear again the next night, and when I looked out just before ten, there he was. It became almost a ritual,

looking out and watching him go by. My son used to tease
me about it, saying I was silly, imagining things about who
he might be, what he might do, and one thing and another. I
thought up all sorts of things about him and who he might
be. A voyeur, a mysterious avenger, a mugger or a drug ped-
dler...everything. It was quite exciting. If you're that
interested, my son used to say, why don't you go and find
out who he is and what he does? But that would have
spoiled the fun. I mean, if I'd known who he was and that
he was on a perfectly legitimate errand, that would have
been the end of the mystery. But now...now he's obviously disappeared, I really want to know who he was and what
he did. Supposing I was right? Supposing he was a little mad,
or there was something fishy about him? My husband used
to get annoyed with me on weekends, always going over to
the window to look. Being a nosy parker, as he put it. He'll
be glad the man's gone and I've lost my evening's entertain-
ment. He hasn't been home since the man stopped coming.
He said once he would put a stop to it, threatening to go out
and take the man by the scruff of his neck and find out who
the hell he was and what he thought he was doing. But I
managed to stop him. That would have been dreadful,
wouldn't it?''

Werner and Alec thought she was a chatterbox.

They were all three standing on the corner now.

The door to the police station opened and an ash-blond
man came out without an overcoat on, his hands in his
trouser pockets. He wove his way through the traffic and
came over to them.

''Good morning,'' he said. ''So it's you playing at detec-
tives, is it? I might have known.''

''Sorry?'' said Werner.

''A woman phoned from down the street to report some
bogus policemen going around asking questions. She said
they looked peculiar and were probably out to rob her. I
realized it must be you. Have you set up some kind of detective corps?''

''These are two acquaintances who are also interested.''

''So you are not giving up?''

''No,'' said Soderstrom. ''There seems to be no reason to.
As long as the police won't do anything, then ordinary
people like us have to try to do what we can.''

Elg rolled his eyes. ''Well, I can't stop you. But you really
mustn't pester people.''

"We only ask politely if anyone knows anything."

"And what have you found out?"

"Well, not much."

"So he doesn't live on Maria Street?"

"No."

Elg looked around.

"Are you going to try Bridge Street or Park Street or Sorans Street? Then there are all the cross streets, too." He laughed and went on, "Wouldn't it be better to put an ad in the papers? Wanted: mysterious man. God, it's cold. Let me know if you find anything, won't you?"

"If anything's happened to him, you'll be the first to know."

"After you, yes."

"Perhaps it'll be too late by then," said Alec, annoyed by the policeman's attitude.

"Huh," said Elg, then muttering something he went back into the warmth of the police station.

"What was he muttering about?" said Barbara.

"I don't know, but it wasn't polite," said Alec. "What now?"

"Hmm," said Werner, scratching his chin.

He considered their various alternatives.

"That's the question," he said. "The paper comes out tomorrow, doesn't it?"

"I think so," said Alec. "Why?"

"That policeman gave me an idea...but what do we do now? Go that way? Or that way? Or that way?"

They stood there irresolutely. They were cold.

Barbara suggested they go back to her place and warm themselves up with some coffee. And a drink.

THE MAN WHO CAME to the offices of the *Daily News* had red spots of cold on his cheeks and smelled of drink. He was a powerful man, and when he took off his fur hat it could be seen that he was bald. His face was fat, too, with pendulous cheeks. His hands were huge and rough. He asked to speak to someone, saying his name was Werner Soderstrom.

Walter Astrom, the local editor, was hunched over his typewriter working on his annual column. With his two forefingers he had typed ONCE MORE THE TURN OF THE YEAR as a headline for his article, which he was already halfway through and which had started:

Confronting another year is like coming to another milestone in life. An important moment. The years go by and thus we notice how our life on this earth is bounded by time. A year passes quickly and the closing of the account always shows a varied menu. Looking around locally, for us in Himmelsholm, 1977 has not been the most joyful of years.

He frowned irritably and reluctantly raised his eyes from his opus when someone knocked on the door.

Soderstrom came in and looked around.

"Yes?" said Astrom.

"I was directed here. You're the editor, is that right?"

"I am," said Astrom, leaning back and looking at him. "What's it about?"

"I thought perhaps your paper might help. It's about someone who's disappeared."

"That's more a police matter, isn't it?"

"Yes, but—"

"Well, I haven't time. One of my colleagues will have to see to it. I'm busy at the moment. Go into the next room. There's someone there called Borg. Talk to him, then we can talk about it later . . . if it's anything for the paper."

"All right," said Soderstrom, retreating.

Astrom looked at the closed door and wrinkled his nose. He thought he could smell drink, and that reminded him that he must remember to buy some for Christmas.

"Where was I now?" he said aloud.

Then he went on typing,

Another year . . . what do people think? Naturally we can wish for better things in 1978. We can have hopes, hopes for peace in our relationships, a calm and uneventful year. We can have faith in all the best things during the year to come. But the gap between wishes and reality we all know is a wide one. The new year remains a blank page and the prelude to it can hardly be described as favorable.

He scratched in his ear and nodded with satisfaction. Now he'd picked up the thread again. He felt a certain sadness. Nineteen-seventy-eight was the year in which he was to retire, but he was going to continue these annual columns for the paper. He had already arranged that with head office.

BO BORG WAS LAUGHING his way through Astrom's column for
the twenty-third of December when Soderstrom knocked
on the door and came in. The column was about how everyone should think about other people at Christmas.

Borg thought Astrom was a pathetic case and a good
example of a journalist who couldn't write. Worst of all,
Borg thought, were Astrom's book reviews, especially when
in his own awful prose he criticized the author's style of
writing.

Borg was in a good mood when Soderstrom came in. He
always was after reading Astrom's column. As soon as he
heard what Soderstrom had to say, he was filled with
enthusiasm and desire for action.

"Don't know whether we can write it up," he said.

"You, too," sighed Soderstrom. "Do people have to die
before the police or the newspapers take an interest? For
Christ's sake."

"No, no, don't misunderstand me. But if I write something about this. . . along the lines of a mysterious disappearance or something like that, and then it turns out it
isn't mysterious at all, there'll be hell to pay. The man
might—"

"Now, look here. I'm sure there's something odd about
his disappearance!" said Soderstrom loudly, banging his fist
on the desk. "Something bloody well must be done. Who in
the hell can I turn to? If neither the police nor the papers
can do anything, who the hell do I speak to? The parson?"

Borg laughed.

"No," he said. "I'll see what I can do."

He looked at the notes he'd been making while Soderstrom had been talking and reckoned he could read most of
them.

"What did he look like? The description's a bit vague."

"Nobody really knows. All I know is that he walks rather
bowed, sort of loping along, has a beard and smokes
cigarillos."

Borg nodded.

"I'll do what I can."

"Thanks," said Soderstrom. "I'll go on looking. There are
three of us now. But it isn't easy. . . like looking for a needle
in a haystack."

Borg nodded.

"Happy Christmas," said Soderstrom as he left.

Borg propped his elbows on his desk.

If he told Astrom all that, he would never be allowed to write about it. He dialed the head-office number in the neighboring town and asked to speak to the chief editor, who gave his consent.

Borg felt considerable excitement as he put a piece of paper into his typewriter, wondering whether he ought to get a picture of the street in, too. There should be one in the picture archives. Otherwise he'd have to fix a photographer.

9

THE MAN

THE ALARM WAS GIVEN at seventeen minutes to four in the afternoon.

The woman's voice on the phone was shrill and hysterical.

"He's dead!" she cried. "He's. . . I went down to the yard to put some rubbish in the bin and then I saw him. He was dead! Blood all over him!"

The woman began to cry.

They managed to get her to give her name and address, then the message was passed on to the Crime Division. Seved Olofsson told Holmberg and Mansson. They went in an unmarked car, but it had a siren and they put it full on. They were in a hurry.

"Could it be her husband?" said Holmberg.

"We'll see," said Olofsson.

"Just before Christmas and all," muttered Mansson, lighting a cigarette.

They were subdued, seeing their Christmas taken up with a murder case.

Two patrol cars were parked outside the apartment house, their rotary lights flashing. The usual curious crowd had flocked around and groups of people were watching from neighboring windows.

The patrol-car crews were standing by one of the cars, talking to each other, looking confused and helpless.

Holmberg switched off and braked in behind them. One of the uniformed men waved a welcome to him.

"Where is he?" said Olofsson. "Have you sent for an ambulance?"

"No. More like the dog wagon needed."

"What?"

"You won't believe your own eyes," said the policeman. "Come and look."

They trooped into the yard.

It was a small stone yard with a tall tree growing by one

wall, and a neat row of garbage bins at the far end alongside
something like a toolshed. The snow was red over there.
But they had to go over to the bin to see the battered
corpse. Not until they had got right up to it and lifted the
lid could they see it. The head was almost severed from
the body, presumably with a knife. One leg was at an
angle that showed it was broken, and the head also looked
as if it had been attacked. One eye socket was empty. The
other eye was staring straight at death, the tongue hanging
three-quarters of the way out of the mouth. One ear was
missing and the caked blood indicated that it had been cut
off.

"God Almighty!" said Mansson.

"Well?" said the uniformed man. "You didn't expect
that, did you?"

"Stop talking like a bloody conjurer who's managed to
stick the sawn-off lady together without any glue. Can any
of you tell me how you examine the site of the crime in a
case like this?"

Holmberg rubbed his chin uncertainly.

"Whose dog is it?" he said. "Is it the woman's...the one
who phoned us?"

"No," said the policeman.

"We'll have to talk to her all the same. Where does she
live?"

"Third floor up. Through that door there. But what do we
do with the body?"

"Are the technical boys on their way?"

"Yes, they should be."

"Well, they'd better take some pictures. See if they can
find anything useful. There may be some clue, but I doubt
it. Come on, boys, let's go and talk to...what's her name?"

"Brostrom."

"God Almighty!" Mansson said again, shaking his head.
"Hell...a dog! I've seen a lot in my day, but that just about
takes the biscuit."

Britta Brostrom was twenty-three years old, and her large
breasts were out of proportion with her thin body. She had
coal-black hair down to her waist, a pointed nose and thin
face.

"It was silly of me to be so hysterical," she said. "But it
was such a shock when I saw it. I didn't know what to do. So
I called the police."

"You were quite right to do that," said Olofsson.
"Haven't you any idea whose dog it is?"

"No. Wall lives one floor up and he's got a dog, but that's a terrier."

"As far as you know, then, it didn't belong to anyone in this apartment house?" said Olofsson.

She shook her head. "No one here owns it."

"Do you know anyone in the street who owns an Alsatian?" said Holmberg.

"No, not that I can remember."

"So you went down to the bin to throw away . . . what?"

"The rubbish."

"And when you got to the bin, what did you do?"

"I was about to lift the lid when I saw the dog. I just went crazy, and ran back in again. Then I phoned the police. It was the only thing I could think of doing."

"Funny no one else saw him," said Holmberg, going over to the window. "Or her."

"It's a she," said Mansson. "I saw."

"Oh, yes," said Holmberg looking out.

From where he was standing he could see one paw sticking out.

"I'm probably the only one here."

"Where are all the others?"

"Not that many live here. Five apartments. Kurt and May have gone away for Christmas. They're sociology students. So are Sven and Matt. They've gone home for Christmas, too. Vanya is at work and Ulf's in the hospital. I'm the only one at home."

"What do you do? Are you a student or . . . ?"

"Yes. English literature."

Olofsson nodded.

"And of course you've neither seen nor heard anything that might have anything to do with it?"

"No, nothing. All I know is that I went down and there it was. How awful! I mean, supposing that had been done to a person? It's frightening even to think about it. Who could do such a thing? He must be crazy. Some sick person. Thank heavens I'm going away tomorrow."

"To your parents?"

She nodded.

AN HOUR AND A HALF LATER they were sitting in Olofsson's room.

"We must talk to that Vanya Muller, of course," said Holmberg. "She might have heard something last night.

Though I doubt she saw anything. She'd have been as scared as the other girl."

"The dog wasn't killed there," said Mansson. "There would've been much more blood around."

"Yes," said Holmberg. "It was killed somewhere else and then tipped behind the bins. Why just that yard?"

"Chance, perhaps?"

"But the dog must've been killed relatively close by. I can't see anyone lugging a dead dog any distance in that state."

"But there's no one in the street who owned an Alsatian."

"The dog must have belonged in the neighborhood. Wonder what happened to its collar? Whether it fell off or whoever did it took it away."

"I suppose we must trace the owner," sighed Olofsson.

"Surely it's damned silly to start all that just for a dog. Sooner or later someone'll miss it, surely? This evening, if not sooner, and the owner will make himself known."

"If he hears how the dog was killed, yes."

"So long as it wasn't the owner who did it."

"If I had a dog I could never bring myself to do such a thing," said Olofsson. "God, a dog's like a member of the family. No one could do that to anyone in his family."

"If you're insane you can do anything," said Mansson.

"Here," said Holmberg, pushing a pin into the wall map. "That's where the dog was found in the yard. According to what we know, there's no one on Cross Street who has an Alsatian. But if the dog was taken there—even by car—it makes sense to start by concentrating in the Frenne Street, Hospital Street, Maria Street and Garden Street area."

The fifteen men from three different squads of the Crime Division did not relish having to cooperate on Operation-Knocking-on-Doors for the sake of a dog.

They were all hoping they'd be able to trace the owner as soon as possible, so that they would not have to spend Christmas Eve on such an unrewarding task. In fact the whole operation was abandoned only ten minutes later.

Lars Westerberg discovered that the expression "third time lucky" had something in it.

Mansson had persisted in the idea that the killing of the dog might have something to do with drugs. Some ex-addicts were nowadays equipped with large dogs that commanded respect, for the simple reason that the dog acted as a weapon when it came to staving off the pushers, who liked to see reformed drug takers going back to their old habits again. But the dog owner was not a drug addict.

The first person Westerberg called on had no idea if anyone in Maria Street owned an Alsatian, so he went down one floor and was told there that the blind man on the ground floor owned one.

It was soon clear to Westerberg that he had come to the right place. The dead Alsatian had been Martin Bard's guide dog, Queenie. But it took a long time for Olofsson, Holmberg and Westerberg to persuade Bard that Queenie was dead.

"Can I feel her coat to make sure?" he said.

Olofsson sighed.

"Later," he said. "We'll try to arrange it. But tell us how the dog got out."

"May—that's my sister—went to work at seven o'clock as usual this morning, and Queenie went with her, as usual. She used to go with her as far as the corner and then come home again when she'd done her morning business. But sometimes she went all the way to the kiosk with May and stayed there until both of them came back. On days when I couldn't or didn't want to go out. Like today, for instance. My cold's too bad for me to go out today. So Queenie has probably gone with May. I knew that when she didn't scratch at the door to come in. They'll be back soon, I should think."

"Queenie is dead." Holmberg reminded him quietly.

The unseeing eyes seemed to be looking at a point alongside him.

"I won't believe that until I've felt her coat," he insisted stubbornly.

May came back a few minutes later. Olofsson had sent a patrol car to fetch her from the kiosk where she worked.

When May came in without Queenie, then Bard understood. The blind man's eyes filled with tears and an expression of hatred and incomprehension came into them.

"But why, why?" said May. "Everyone liked Queenie. The children here loved playing with her. Who could have done such a thing to us?"

"What happened this morning?" said Olofsson. "The dog went with you, is that right?"

"Yes, to the corner of South Esplanade. But then I patted her and told her to go home."

"Sometimes she went with you and stayed at the kiosk with you. Didn't she do that today?"

"No."

"Why not?"

May shrugged. "She didn't want to."

"But presumably you and your brother agreed over whether she would go with you or come back here," said Holmberg.

"No, *she* decided," said Bard.

"Shut your mouth," said May. "He's talking rubbish," she explained to Holmberg.

"But what did happen?"

"Sometimes she sent Queenie home and sometimes she didn't."

"Did the dog often stay with you at the kiosk?"

"No. Only when my brother wasn't well enough to go out and had to stay at home. He's not strong, but it makes no difference how bad he is, he always wants to go out. Even when he's got a streaming cold and it's pouring outside. I've had to be a mother to him. Almost a nursemaid."

Holmberg looked at them, the blind man huddled up in his chair, picking at the arm of it, May irritably looking at her brother, blinking over and over again.

They were both in their forties, both rather short, both very fat. The atmosphere between them was loaded.

"Has your brother any enemies?" said Holmberg.

"No, I'm sure he hasn't. He hates people, hates mixing with them. He doesn't want anything to do with them. He's never got to know anyone well enough to make enemies."

"Who should I mix with? With you out at your kiosk most of the time. You meet people, but I have to sit here alone. The only pleasure I had was going out with Queenie—but now I can't even do that any longer. And you're hardly ever home in the evenings. I suppose you've got some man somewhere."

"Oh, shut your mouth. You know I go to my classes. Don't sit there talking filth about me in front of other people."

"What usually happens in the daytime?" said Olofsson.

"He—" May started.

"I was asking your brother," said Olofsson, interrupting her sharply.

"Huh!" snorted May.

"I wake up, and if she's let Queenie stay at home we go for a walk after I've had my breakfast. And then another in the afternoon. That's it. You wake up, eat, go for a walk, go home and eat, go for a walk, go home, eat, sit and listen to the radio in the evening."

"Haven't you any friends you go and see sometimes?"

He shook his head slowly.

"No one you meet on your walks?"

"No."

"Don't you ever meet anyone and stop and talk?"

"No."

Holmberg had the impression that Bard was slightly backward. He looked around the crowded apartment. One room was his sister's, everything in it in perfect order. The other room was his and was spartan. Then there was a living room containing a great jumble of furniture. Holmberg wondered how a blind man could move around in it.

"Have you never quarreled with anyone?"

"No."

"But you must know someone?"

"No."

"He's a loner."

"I want to look after myself. I would if she'd only let me. But she always wants to decide everything."

"Have you ever had a burglary?" Mansson asked.

"No!" said the sister.

"Do you know anyone who might have been annoyed by the dog?"

"No—"

"How will I get out for my walk now?" Bard interrupted plaintively. "I'll have to get another dog, but how... Queenie...."

He was sitting with his mouth hanging open, apparently utterly resigned.

"Miss Bard," said Holmberg. "Is there something about the death of the dog that you're hesitating about telling us?"

"No," she said emphatically.

"Who did you meet today on your way to the kiosk?"

"No one."

He looked at her.

"What time do you open the kiosk?"

"Eight."

"Does it take a whole hour to walk there?"

"No, I go to church on my way."

"Church?"

"She imagines she's religious," said Bard. "She prays every morning."

"Shut your mouth, you blasphemous heathen."

"If God made me blind, he could give me back my sight, couldn't he?"

Is he backward, thought Holmberg. Or is he just cowed and afraid of her? And daring to speak because we're here?

"How did you become blind? Was it an accident?" he asked.

"No, my sight just went. I'd always had poor sight, but when I was only fifteen, one day it just went altogether."

"And now I have to look after him," said May.

She snorted and stamped her foot.

The corners of his mouth twitched.

Holmberg thought, she wouldn't dare hit him, would she? Not as long as the dog was there.

"The dog was all I had," he said quietly. "And you tried to take that away from me, too. You tried to make her yours."

"I've never heard anything so stupid. Don't listen to him. He's not—well, you know. . . ."

He was looking straight ahead and smiling.

Holmberg shook his head and looked at Olofsson, who was looking pained.

"Do you want us to find out who did that to Queenie?" Holmberg said.

Bard started and sat up straighter, then relaxed and hunched up again. He began to cry quite silently.

May said nothing, showing nothing.

"In that case," Holmberg went on, "it's important that you help us by telling us everything you know . . . about enemies . . . if you have any suspicions . . . if you—"

"I don't know anything," said May, sitting down at last. "I don't know anything."

She sounded as if she were telling the truth.

"How did she die?" Bard asked.

They had kept that from him, but now Leif Mansson told him.

Martin Bard clenched his fists and screamed. May put her hands over her ears and she screamed, too.

"It's not true! It's not true!" she cried. "Queenie! Oh, Queenie!"

"I JUST DON'T GET IT," said Mansson in the car on their way back. "It doesn't make sense."

That was roughly what they all thought.

They hadn't the slightest idea why the dog had had to die, least of all why so cruelly. Or who could have done such a thing.

"She *couldn't* have had anything to do with it," said Olofsson.

"No, of course not," said Holmberg dispiritedly. "Didn't you see how fond of the dog she was?"

THE OTHER MAN

Putting his thoughts and reflections down in writing had become a habit he had developed over the years. He was sitting there now with a pencil in his mouth, chewing on it as he looked at his own face in the mirror.

He had grown fat over the years.

No, only recently.

Yes, actually fat.

It wasn't only irregular meals. It was the lack of exercise, too, and then alcohol was also fattening.

He sighed.

Then he put pen to paper and wrote:

It isn't only those born dead who are dead. We so-called living are also born dead. As all of us will die, there's nothing really to live for. It seems hardly worth it, least of all if one has nothing to live for.

He thought, I wonder if anyone will ever read these notes? What will they think then?

He wondered what it was he had started.

But there was no way back now.

Because now he had begun the end.

THE MAN

THEY DIDN'T SEEM TO BE getting any further with the dog murder. They had been back to Maria Street and made inquiries about Martin Bard and his sister. They had spoken to people to find out whether the brother and sister had any enemies, whether there was anyone who hated the dog for some reason, or who had reason to wish the brother and sister harm by attacking the dog.

But they had found nothing.

Few people in the neighborhood knew the Bards and none were friendly with them. No one stopped to exchange a few words with either of them. The general impression was that they wished to be left alone. Martin seemed shy and awkward, and May was clearly a chatterbox whose main subject of conversation was moans about her own life.

It seemed to be generally accepted that they were two isolated people who were attached to each other, but their retiring nature was to some extent of their own choosing. No one had ever noticed any hostility between them, nor had any loud quarrels between them been heard through the walls of their apartment. Generally speaking, no one knew anything about them whatsoever, except that they existed and lived where they lived.

The blind man had been seen on his slow walks with Queenie. The sister had often been seen leaving home in the evenings, but she always returned home around nine.

And the dog. . . general opinion was that it was in every respect an extraordinary creature, a real personality with a strongly developed individuality.

Several people used to meet the dog in the mornings on her way back after parting on the corner from May, and some had seen them parting there. May always hugged Queenie and the dog lovingly licked her face and hands. Then they went off in their different directions. . . May to work and Queenie home.

That was if the dog didn't go on with her. Then they saw them walking quickly side by side, the plump May waddling along, the dog gracefully padding beside her. They knew Bard wouldn't go out on those days.

Otherwise, it was the usual sight of the blind man and his guide dog. They often went for walks, and there was a kind of glow around the dog, as if she radiated ownership. You did not get the impression that the blind man owned the dog, but that it was the dog who was Bard's master.

Queenie looked as if she was showing off her favorite pup, the proud mother out for a walk.

Everyone had respected the dog and the children had loved her. No one could imagine how on earth anyone could have done such a thing to Queenie.

Bard seemed to come second; no one gave a thought to what it all meant to him.

They shook their heads and said that it affected them as it would have done if it had been a person.

"It can't have been all that easy to kill a great strong Alsatian like that," said Westerberg. "I mean, dogs like that are powerful and can defend themselves. And not everyone can get close to such a dog. If someone went for her, meaning to do her harm, the dog would have known instinctively there was danger ahead, and would have defended herself . . . probably attacked."

"So you think the person who killed the dog must have been someone who knew her?" said Olofsson.

Westerberg pursed his lips and looked thoughtful.

"It's a thought," he said.

"Is your argument," said Mansson, "that we've perhaps already been in contact with whoever did it? That it might be one of the people living along the street—someone we've talked to?"

Westerberg flung out his arms.

"I don't know," he said. "But I'd like to see the person who could have done that without knowing the dog at all."

"It's like a bad detective story," muttered Holmberg. "All the circumstances point to the victim recognizing his murderer and letting him into his apartment, offering him sherry and then being stabbed in the back as he turned around to get out cigars for him."

"I'm going crazy," said Olofsson. "This is just as complicated as it would've been if it had been a person."

"But *where* was it killed?" sighed Mansson. "There must be blood wherever it was killed."

"You'd think so," said Westerberg. "But we didn't find any anywhere."

"And no one's seen anything," said Olofsson quietly, getting up from his chair.

He went over to the window and looked out. It was getting dark, the sky clear, the stars just beginning to emerge.

"No one's seen anything," he repeated.

"Someone saw May and Queenie walking along the street," said Holmberg.

"Yes, but that's all. No one saw them part on the corner. No one saw the dog return. No one heard a car. No one heard a dog barking. Is there anyone around there who's known to have been violent before?"

"Not that I know of," said Mansson. "Do you mean violence against people?"

"Yes—adults, children or animals. There are people who like tormenting other living creatures."

Olofsson sat down again and propped his elbows on the chair arms, leaning his head on one hand as he tapped the other thumbnail lightly against his front teeth.

"The question is, what on earth can we do about it?" he said quietly.

There had been a palpable air of unease and oppression all down Maria Street. The people they had talked to had shuddered and looked frightened when they heard what had happened. It was all so incomprehensible and impossible to grasp.

And so terrifying.

WHEN MARTIN HOLMBERG got home, Kerstin was in low spirits. He noticed at once as soon as he stepped through the door and saw her standing there with the telephone receiver in her hand.

THE OTHER MAN

IT WAS THE EVENING before Christmas Eve and now they were four. Bo Borg had joined them.

When he had finished his article, he had phoned Soderstrom to read it over to him to be sure he had the facts correct. That was unusual for him. Usually he relied entirely on his notes, his memory and his own judgment.

"Are you going to go on looking?" he had asked.

"Yes, indeed. We're meeting opposite the police station at five o'clock."

Soderstrom was extremely surprised when Borg appeared.

"I was curious," he said.

Soderstrom introduced Borg to Alec Svensen and Barbara Johansson.

"You haven't spoken to the police by any chance, have you?" said Svensen. "I mean, as a newspaperman, you've a better chance of putting pressure on them."

"I had a word with Elg, yes—he's the one you saw. But he said roughly the same to me as he did to you. And he said you were an obstinate devil," Borg added with a smile.

Soderstrom looked at the police station across the road and frowned.

"There they are, sitting in there," he said. "They should be out here looking. But what's the use of getting annoyed about it? If we're to get anywhere, we'd better be off. What're we going to do?"

Bridge Street was to their left, Sorans Street and Park Street to their right. Behind them was Maria Street, and then there were all the cross streets.

"The possibilities are enormous," said Alec. "But we've got to start somewhere."

"We have started," said Werner. "Now we've got to go on."

Barbara looked around but said nothing.

Bo looked around, then took his pipe out of his duffel-coat pocket and slowly and carefully began to fill it.

"If he came from that direction," he said pointing the pipe stem, "why did he come right around here? Why didn't he go through the park? He seems to have walked around the park."

"Exactly," said Alec. "Perhaps he didn't dare walk through the park that late. When you think what goes on there. There've been one or two attacks."

"You've asked at all the apartments around the crossroads, haven't you?" Bo said quickly. "Had anyone seen which way he turned off?"

"We haven't asked everyone," said Werner. "But those we did ask said no."

"Supposing," said Bo, "the people in the windows facing the park saw him coming and going. Supposing they stayed there for a while to see if he went along Sorans Street or Park Street, because you must be able to see those streets from the windows nearest the crossroads. Presumably they would also have seen whether he came from that direction before he turned off onto Maria Street...in which case, they would have said so. That he came from that direction or went in that direction, I mean."

"Yes," said Alec. "You're right there."

"So," said Borg, pointing his pipe toward Bridge Street, "he probably came from that direction...and went back in that direction."

South Square was down there, and if one walked in that direction one came south of the town center. There the alternatives were endless, as there were a great many streets and also a great many tall blocks full of apartments. All around the square and along the streets radiating from it were residential blocks.

"I'm beginning to think we're not going to get much further," sighed Werner. "Perhaps the whole thing's a crazy idea."

It would have been ideal if the man had come from the other direction, because the apartment blocks there were fewer and smaller, and the streets fewer, too.

"We can't give up," said Alec. "Not now."

"But will we get any further?" said Barbara. "And it's cold."

"I know!" said Bo, trying to snap his fingers in gloves. "I've got it!"

"What?" said Werner.

"Come on," said Bo, setting off toward the square.

The square had originally been a field. When Himmels-holm became a town and began to expand at the beginning of the First World War, the field had been a muddy place for cattle. In the twenties the cattle market had been closed and the grass began to grow again. In the thirties the market was asphalted over and a drinking fountain put in the middle. In the fifties it became the business center, and the square was the central forum on Sundays. In the sixties department stores were built around Great Square to the north, and toward the end of the decade South Square had begun to get a bad reputation and was where gangs of youngsters met with their battered cars. Now in the seventies people had again started walking around there after dark. There was a snack bar on the corner between Bridge Street and Town Hall Street.

In 1946 Sievert Hansson had begun to sell hot dogs with or without rolls, plus a special kind of mustard from a little stall he pulled there every evening.

Sievert Hansson was an institution. He was called Hot Dog Harry and in '46 he had described his occupation as a "hot-dog vendor." Thirty-one years later he called himself "managing director." Nowadays he had a wide selection on his menu to choose from, because nowadays Hot Dog Harry sold more than sausages and hamburgers. You could buy mild beer and soft drinks, milkshakes or fruit juices. You could buy cigarettes or cigarillos or cigars. You could even buy condoms, but the sale of these was not what it used to be on Saturday nights in the forties and fifties . . . then prospective customers had leaned confidentially across the counter and discreetly whispered what they wished to buy.

The snack bar on the corner was now a small shop. Hot Dog Harry was not pleased with the development. At various stages he had been forced to improve his hot-dog stall, starting when the health authorities made him immobilize it, as mobile stalls were no longer allowed. Then they had said he should get a refrigerator. When he was told that he would have to install a lavatory, he had the whole hot-dog kiosk torn down and built a snack bar on the street along American lines   a hot dog palace, he called it.

No, things had been better before when his little white stall had been sufficient. He sold the same hot dogs, didn't he? But now he cooked them in a variety of ways.

Hot Dog Harry was no friend of development. He had lived through the idyllic forties, the intellectual fifties, then the bike-boy and car-gang sixties, and now the glossy welfare seventies.

Hot Dog Harry knew a great many people and everyone knew Hot Dog Harry.

At first he had been a hot-dog vendor who liked chatting with as many customers as possible, a small man who liked to warm himself with a nip or two when it was cold. But as the old white stall became a yellow hot-dog kiosk and then a red snack bar with flashing neon lighting, Hot Dog Harry's prestige also rose.

Now he was managing director.

Despite his title, he looked after all sales himself.

His speech was rich, if by rich was meant that it was spiced with oaths. Members of the free churches in the town were not Hot Dog Harry's customers. Perhaps he had lost much good custom in them, for the square contained two tabernacles, the Pentecostal Church and the Bethlehem Chapel.

It was said that Hansson the Managing Director had been married since the thirties, but no one had ever seen his wife, and she had never assisted him at either the stall, the kiosk or the snack bar.

It was to this hot-dog merchant that Bo took his companions that evening.

There was a line outside the snack bar, people laden with parcels and Christmas trees staving off the worst of their hunger before going home for their evening meal.

Bo stood in the line. There were seven people in front of him.

"Are you going to buy a hot dog?" asked Werner.

"No. But if anyone knows anything about the people around here, Hot Dog Harry does."

Bo Borg had lived in town for only four years, but during that time he had found out almost everything worth knowing about. And Hot Dog Harry was among the most worthwhile people in town to know.

At last it was his turn.

"Hi!" he said.

Sievert glanced up. He looked tired.

"Hi," he said. "Every bloody man jack seems to want hot dogs tonight. What the hell do you want?"

"Nothing, thanks, but I'd like to ask you something."

"Oh, go to hell, you young bum. Do you think I've time to stand here talking?"

"I'll be quick."

The man behind Bo cleared his throat loudly.

"It's important," said Bo.

"There's a line behind you. What the hell do you want to know? Quick now."

Sievert was stout and more or less circular, with a small round nose and a square face.

"Not too easy to explain," said Bo.

"Come on now, bloody hurry up. People want hot dogs."

"Can't I come in behind? Then I can explain while you're serving your customers."

Sievert shrugged and then grimaced resignedly, which meant he smoothed out the whole of his furrowed old face as he jerked his thumb at the door and turned to the man behind Bo.

The line was now snaking outside the kiosk. Hot dogs and hamburgers and all the other satisfying goodies from Hot Dog Harry's hands were served across the counter with the speed of a conveyer belt, and the change clattered.

Werner, Alec and Barbara stood outside fighting off the cold, watching through the glass as Bo gesticulated and explained his errand.

"Yes," said Sievert, "I know the guy you mean."

He spread a thick layer of mustard onto half a chicken, muttering something about barbaric eating habits before handing it to the customer and taking the money.

"He came here every night and bought a hot dog," he said, stirring the mustard before spreading it along a sausage.

"At what time?"

"Half-past ten. On the dot. I could've set my watch by him. What sort of mustard did you say?" he said to the customer.

"Do you know who he is?"

"No, I haven't got any fish mustard! Yes, of course I do."

"Who is he, then? What's his name?"

"No, hell, go and buy pizzas somewhere else. There are limits! Name? I don't know his name."

"What do you know about him? Apart from that he bought a hot dog from you regularly."

"He lived somewhere over there, that I do know."

He inclined his head in a southerly direction.

"Down toward Town Hall Street?"

"Yes. Three mineral waters, wasn't it? Mineral water! What sort of drink is that? He went off in that direction, anyhow."

"Did you ever speak to him?"

"Of course. I mean, he's been coming here night after night since '72—Happy Christmas to you, too, madam—so of course we talked."

"What about?"

"Nothing special. He came and bought a grilled sausage with a roll and south-country mustard, then ate it. Then we exchanged a few words and he left when he'd finished."

"He never said anything to indicate who he was or what he did or where he came from?"

"No. But he seemed educated."

"What do you mean?"

"He used fancy words—once said something about schools."

"What did he say?"

"That it wasn't easy to work in today's schools."

"Was he a teacher, do you think?"

"Wouldn't surprise me. He seemed very quiet and timid."

"Did he wear a wedding ring?"

"No," said Sievert without hesitation. "Don't you want a hot dog, now you're here?"

"For free?"

"Are you crazy? With the cost of things today? He was wearing mourning a year or two back."

"When?"

"Two years ago."

"What did he look like?"

"High forehead. Intelligent people have that, don't they? And a beard. Straight nose and blue eyes. Long fingers, too, and they'd never been used for hard work. No, an educated man. A bookish man. Wouldn't surprise me if he was a teacher."

Sievert straightened his cap and puffed. He put some more sausages on the grill.

"Wasn't he ever with anyone else?"

"No, and he wasn't talkative, either. But he complained about his rotten view sometimes."

"What?"

"He said it was so damned boring having a view over a bloody sports stadium."

THAT LIMITED THE FIELD.

They were standing on the sidewalk, behind them the
fence that ran around the old sports stadium where so many
memorable ice-hockey matches had been played at the time
when the town team had been its pride and joy. The only
apartment houses in Town Hall Street with a view over the
old stadium were the two red roofed five-story blocks on
the other side.

"So he must live in one of those," said Bo.

Werner sighed.

"Must be at least fifty people in each one," he said. "Both
have two entrances and at least two or three apartments
per floor."

"Don't sound so downhearted. We're much nearer now."

"So near and yet so far away," sighed Alec.

"Nonsense," said Bo. "Four stairways. There must be
someone in one of them who can tell us where he lives."

"It's seems almost wrong," said Werner. "Suddenly I
don't want to find him."

"Whatever next?" said Barbara.

"You sound like a child whose toys have been taken away,"
said Bo, laughing. "Come on, let's take a stairway each."

They went in. They rang every single doorbell on all four
stairways.

When they were again gathered on the sidewalk, they
were as irresolute as ever.

They had one apartment house behind them. To their left
was the square, to the right Town Hall Street ran past two
filling stations, and it was quite a distance to the next apartment house. Straight ahead of them was the old stadium,
pale lights floodlighting the ice crowded with skaters, the
villas in the darkness on the other side of the stadium only
just visible.

"Well, that's that," sighed Bo. "and it all seemed so
promising."

"What do we do now, then?" said Alec.

"I'm going home," said Barbara. "I must go and do something about Christmas."

"Oh, hell," said Werner.

The man did not live on any of the four stairways.

"I give up," he said. "For tonight, anyhow. Perhaps the
newspaper tomorrow will . . . ."

So they parted without settling on another meeting the
following day.

Bo Borg was thoughtful as he walked home.

Mixed with his thoughts of the mystery man, as he called him, were his thoughts of Monica Hubertsson, blond, slim, beautiful and young, but engaged to someone else.

Bo Borg was feeling lonely, as he had done for the whole of the four years he'd lived in Himmelsholm.

This town makes you chronically lonely, he thought. I wonder if the mystery man is that kind of lonely person?

When his loneliness was too much to bear, he often went hopefully into the bar in the hotel in Great Square. Sometimes a waitress there would go back home with him. She was about forty-four and he thought her skin was a bit rough. But she had a desperate appetite for life and complemented perfectly Bo Borg's need to kill his loneliness.

He didn't have difficulties making contact with people. It was just that the women he took a liking to all too seldom took a liking to him.

He stopped and looked at the clothes in a shop window.

He found the town suffocating, oppressive.

It was a small town, not even middle-sized by Swedish standards. Distances were short, cliques firmly established, social limitations forming barriers.

Bo Borg longed to get away, mostly back to Lund, but there was no work for him there. He was afraid of getting stuck in Himmelsholm and that he would become like Erik Asker, the sports editor, an embittered bachelor who knew everyone because of his profession, but no one privately, so had few friends, if any.

If I stick it here much longer, he thought, I'll start accepting that this is what life is. He envisaged a lonely man walking along a deserted street, the cold wind hurling snow into his face. The man was hunched up against the wind.

The man looked up and Borg started.

It was himself.

He blinked and hurried off to the hotel bar. As far as he could remember, Berit was working this evening. To hell with the reputation she had.

She was an escape from loneliness and he would not give up the next day until he had found out who the mystery man was, or at least where he came from.

One thing would lead to another, thought Borg, remembering that the next day was Christmas Eve.

THE MAN

IT WASN'T THE LOOK in her eyes as she turned toward him, it was the way she had jumped as he jerked open the door and stepped inside. And the way she had flung down the receiver.

"Thank God you've come home at last! This damned telephone's getting on my nerves. It's been ringing all day—but no one answers!"

He frowned slightly and put his cap up on the hat rack, struggled out of his coat and hung it on a hanger. Then he did the same with his jacket. He loosened his tie, squatted down and untied his laces, pulled off his shoes and thrust his feet into his slippers.

He looked at her.

She looked as if she needed to be hugged.

The children climbed all over him on the floor of the playroom and then twenty minutes later, she told him.

The telephone had rung at ten o'clock. She had just come back after having been down to the shop. She had picked up the receiver to answer, but there had been no one on the other end.

She hadn't thought much about it. Presumably it had been ringing for quite a time and the caller had given up at that moment.

Then it had rung again at eleven o'clock, when she was having coffee in the kitchen with a neighbor.

"I replied, but no one said anything. But I could have sworn someone was there. I heard someone breathing. But then there was a click and the dial tone came back."

He nodded as he lifted a squealing Anders high up into the air.

"Then it went again at twelve. The same thing happened. Then it went at one o'clock. Same again," she said. "Once an hour it's rung and every time the same thing's happened.

I lift up the receiver, no one says anything, there's a click and then the dial tone starts.''

"Funny. Could there be anything wrong with the phone?''

"There must be.''

"It couldn't be a joke, could it?''

"Funny sort of joke, I must say.''

He put the boy down and went downstairs to the telephone. He looked at his watch . . . fifteen seconds to six. He lifted the receiver and heard the dial tone. He put it down. He waited.

The telephone rang.

"Can you get the kids to be quiet!'' he called to Kerstin.

Then he lifted the receiver.

"Hello,'' he said, his voice tense.

"Hello, is that you, Martin?''

"Yes.''

"Hi, it's Boel. Is Kerstin there? I just wanted a word with her. We're looking forward to seeing you on Boxing Day, both of you. Thanks for the Christmas present for Ragnar. I'm sure he'll be thrilled.''

"It's for you!'' he shouted.

While she was talking, he sat down to go through the day's mail, which consisted mostly of Christmas cards. He lighted a cigarette and looked into the darkness outside the kitchen window. Three houses in the row opposite were in darkness.

What was it all about? I must have been woken by the telephone last night. Did I get up? Could there be anything wrong with the phone? But then it wouldn't ring regularly once an hour, would it? Is it one of those damned heavy breathers? I haven't had any dealings with any nut cases recently. What the hell's going on?

Kerstin had finished talking, so he got up, picked up the receiver and put it to his ear. It was warm.

"Who are you calling?''

"Inquiries. I thought I'd find out if there was anything wrong with the phone. . . . Hello, yes. I'm having a bit of trouble with the phone.''

"What's your number?''

He told the operator and after a while was put through to someone else, who showed some interest in settling his problem.

He described fairly fully what had been happening.

"I was wondering if there could be anything wrong with the phone, or something?"

"Yes," said the voice, "there might be. You've no reason to think anyone's playing a joke on you, have you?"

"No."

"May I ask if there might be anyone with a grudge against you who is doing this to get his own back?"

"I don't know."

"I see."

"I wondered whether there could be a technical fault."

"There might be. There are a number of possibilities."

"Could you try to investigate?"

"Tonight?"

"Yes, if possible."

"You'd have to pay for someone to come."

"So this wouldn't be part of the ordinary service?"

"Not at this time of the day. And it's not easy to disconnect the telephone the caller is using. We can, but it could go wrong. The best chance is if we happen to be there the exact moment the phone rings, so we can intervene at once."

"So it's not easy to trace conversations like that?"

"No. There can be quite a number of explanations, as I said. Someone attempting a joke or someone dialing the wrong number and ashamed to admit it. There are all kinds of possibilities."

Martin thought for a moment.

"Of course, if it's unpleasant for you we can disconnect your phone. But there'll be an extra charge "

"No, I can always unplug it here, thanks. No, we'll leave it for the moment I'll come back to you if necessary." He hung up.

"What did they say?" said Kerstin

"Nothing, really. It's probably some fault somewhere, but not that easy to find."

She pushed a strand of hair away from her face and looked at him.

"Martin," she said, answer me honestly. Have you been dealing with someone who might want to get at you in some way?"

He shook his head. it's hard to know. There's always the possibility, the risk. But no one I can think of. Shall I unplug it?"

"If we unplug it, we'll never know if it's stopped."

They left it in.

The telephone did not ring again that evening.

But both Martin and Kerstin kept glancing at it every time they went past it or happened to catch sight of it from the kitchen or the living room. They were feeling uneasy and slightly anxious, perhaps even afraid. Shortly before midnight they crept up to the children's rooms to see whether they were all asleep.

Then they crept out of the house for a short walk before going to bed.

That was nothing unusual. The children practically never woke up and Inger was old enough to see to Anders if he woke, popping the soother in his mouth and telling him to go back to sleep because it was the middle of the night. Inger knew that if she was woken by one of the younger ones crying and neither of her parents could be heard, they were just out for a short walk.

They must have been out for about fifteen minutes. The night was perfectly still, the sky black and the stars brilliant, the snow glittering and crunching under their feet. The air was clean and fresh to breathe. An almost enchanted night.

They could hear the children screaming as they approached the house, their screams apparently echoing in the silence.

THE OTHER MAN

HE HAD NO RECOLLECTION of when he had begun to take an interest in the phenomenon of terrorism. It must have been sometime at the beginning of his own process of disintegration, along with his own defeat as a human being, as an individual, as a person.

The first sign had been a dawning sense of the pointlessness of his own life.

He remembered to a word what he had written in his notebook.

It is extraordinary how stimulating it is to live in the knowledge that perhaps one will experience the disintegration of mankind, perhaps even the world, though it is a pity that there will be no one to tell it to. So what is the use of writing down anything about it for future generations? What generations?

What he was utterly unaware of was the coldness that had settled on him inwardly. It was there, but he was incapable of feeling it. His contempt for his own self became outward contempt, expressed in his way of observing other people and his views on them.

But a flame burned within him that was richly nourished by all that was frozen, his oxygen hopelessness and carbon dioxide contempt; contempt for himself, contempt for the life he was forced to live, contempt for those who forced him to live it, contempt for other people.

That was hatred.

His hatred involved all those who had combined to create the situation he now found himself in, hatred directed against those who lived their apparently happy lives at other people's expense.

Hatred invited action.

He had become interested in the ideology of terrorism, if ideology there was. The idea of terrorism would perhaps be a better way of putting it.

Terrorism, born of hopelessness, despair, loneliness, torment, desperation, oppression. Terrorism created by the supremacy of one's surroundings, by the contempt poured on one.

The idea of terrorism had occasionally seemed to him diffuse and hard to grasp, but he had gradually realized that its most important ingredient when transmitted into action lay in the field of the emotions.

The slow erosion of personality and the ability to feel emotion, the sensation of shrinking as an individual, the devaluation of one as a human being, the total degradation and great loneliness.

He remembered times when he had been ill, but not ill enough to go to a doctor. Colds, short periods, for sure. Some humiliating spells of gastric flu, when he had lain alone in bed and stretched out his hand to the person who did not exist for comfort and help; the person who did not exist to look after him like a child when it has been sick on the floor by the bed and feels much too exhausted and weak to be able to clear it up.

Worst of all were perhaps his thoughts on what his life might have been.

Hatred drove him on.

He picked up his pencil and wrote:

I see mankind, all mankind, as one great creature and that creature is writhing in pain. Its body is burning and sharp thorns prick holes in it. A sticky net surrounds the creature and it howls in its death throes. But death takes a long time and the torment is long and pleasurable. For both; both for the person who suffers and for the person who causes the pain. Now I see myself. And when I see myself, I know who the strong one is.

He put the pencil down and stared vacantly out of the window on the other side of his desk.

He thought, the limits of pain are flexible. At a certain point the borderline is erased and ceases to exist. But the pain remains.

He could see a face in front of him, its contours clear and sharp.

The tears froze to ice and he began to tremble all over. He picked up the paper he had been writing on and crumpled it slowly up into a small hard ball.

He stretched out for the whiskey bottle and almost filled the tooth glass. He drank half of it in one single gulp. At first it burned his throat, but then he was filled with a deceptive warmth.

He clenched his teeth and tried to conjure up that face in his inner vision again.

But the contours were blurred now, and the face melted together with all the rest.

But he knew whose the face was.

He knew who would pay the penalty.

He thought, what were his limits of pain?

Then he suddenly began to laugh.

15

THE MAN

IT TOOK SOME TIME to calm the children down and find out what had happened.

Anders had been woken by the twins' screams, and they had been woken by Inger's scream. The reason was the telephone.

Eventually the ringing of the telephone had woken Inger, and when she realized that no one was answering it, she knew her parents were out for a walk. She had hurriedly got out of bed and gone downstairs to answer it before it woke the others.

"But—but—but there—there—there wasn't anyone there —no one said anything," she sobbed.

No one had spoken, but she had heard a shrill high-pitched laugh, laughter that had sounded inhuman; bellowing ghostlike laughter, like a laughing machine. She had begun to cry and scream uncontrollably.

Martin presumed the laugher had called on the dot of midnight.

They calmed the children down and managed to get them to go to sleep, but Inger insisted on being allowed to creep into her parents' double bed.

Martin and Kerstin sat down in the kitchen, talking in low voices.

"Something terrible is happening," said Kerstin. "It must be some sick person who's out to get at us. Who *could* it be? It must be someone you've had contact with lately, who's decided to take revenge. Has anyone threatened you?"

"There might be someone," he said, running his fingers through his hair. "I mean, it does happen that someone you have to take in, or you have to deal with, says something like, 'I'll get you, you swine.' But you don't take much notice of that. You've heard it so often, and they're mostly drunk or under the influence of drugs. When they sober up they don't remember they've threatened you. Or sometimes it's someone who's been a mental case, but I haven't had anything to do with mental cases for years."

"Could it be anyone who's escaped from St. Lars?"

"I'd have been told if anyone had escaped."

"But supposing they haven't told you? Can't you phone and find out if anyone's escaped . . . someone you had dealings with a long time ago, perhaps?"

"That wouldn't be any use."

She silenced him by putting her hands on top of his and looking at him, her eyes blinking rapidly.

"It's not just you and me," she said. "It's the children, too. . . ."

He nodded and went out to the telephone in the hall.

But the duty officer assured him that no mental hospital in the south of the country had sent out a request for a search for an escaped patient.

"What about the prisons? Do any of their escapees have anything to do with us? Anyone we've arrested or dealt with? Anyone from Lund or—"

"No," the duty officer interrupted him. "No, none. Why are you asking? Has anything happened? Your voice sounds peculiar."

"What? No . . . no, it's nothing. Thanks a lot."

He shook his head in reply to Kerstin's questioning look. He swallowed and dialed the St. Lars number and after persisting for a while he spoke to someone who could assure him that no one had escaped from there. He also called St. Maria's in Helsinborg.

Closing her eyes, Kerstin said quietly, "I wonder if this is going to go on all over Christmas."

"I'll unplug it," he said, doing so. "Then at least we can sleep in peace."

"I don't think I can sleep. I'm frightened, Martin. Frightened."

"You mustn't be."

"But aren't you?"

"Yes. . . ."

He went over to the larder and opened the door of the cupboard at the top. He took out a bottle of whiskey, then took a glass from the cupboard above the sink and poured some out.

"Do you want some?"

She nodded.

He gazed at her as he drank. She was holding the glass against her cheek, looking very tired.

"I'm not really frightened," he said. "Worried, rather...."

He emptied his glass.

"Drink up now, and we'll go to bed."

16

THE OTHER MAN

HE STARTED AND LOOKED AROUND. There was an alien smell in
the room and he was aware that someone was looking at him.

He turned his head.

She was lying on her stomach beside him in the narrow
bed, her elbows propped on the bottom sheet, her head in
her hands. She was looking at him and smiling.

"Did you fall asleep?"

"I must have dozed off . . . what's the time?"

"I don't think I can be bothered to look. Do you know you
look sweet when you're asleep?"

Bo Borg heaved himself up on his elbows, straightened
the pillow, propping it against the wall and leaning against it
as he stretched out his hand. He put it on her head and slowly stroked her hair, then down toward her face. He felt her
forehead with his wrist, then her temples and cheek. He ran
a finger down her nose to her lips.

She smiled, and he felt the trembling of her upper lip
transmitted to his fingertips.

"Berit," he said, running his finger down her cheek.

She closed her eyes and moved her head slightly.

At moments like this, he thought she was beautiful.

"How old are you, actually?" she said abruptly.

"Thirty. Why?"

"How many times have I been back here with you?"

"I don't know."

"Neither do I."

"Does it matter?"

"Not really. But the strange thing is, I know practically
nothing about you. Who are you really, Bo Borg?"

"Who am I? I come from Lund. . . ."

"As if that was an answer to every question. You say that
as if it explained everything. What did you do to land up in
this dump?"

He looked from the desk to the bookcase stuffed with books: novels, a wide range of nonfiction, newspapers and magazines.

One room and a kitchenette.

The bed was a convertible sofa alongside an oval coffee table and the two sagging armchairs needing recovering.

That was all the furniture. A sofa bed, a table, two armchairs, a desk and the overflowing bookcase. He had things stuffed into the built-in wardrobe in the same disorder.

On top of the bookcase was a radio and in one corner on the floor a twelve-inch television set.

"I wanted to be a teacher," he said. "But I didn't get a place at the Institute of Education after university. I tried journalism. I managed to get some temporary jobs in Lund, but nothing permanent. The only permanent post I could find was here at the *Daily News* office in Himmelsholm. I persuade myself I'm being of some use as a journalist. Anyhow, it helps me to survive, financially."

"What kind of use?"

He laughed.

"I take food to the hungry. I try to explain to them what they ought to learn about the society we live in. About this town. I tell them what is happening."

"That's what you think. What do you know about what people ought to know? Or want to know?"

"I don't know," he said truthfully. "Do you know what I'm most scared of? Of getting stuck in this town. Of growing into it. Of not being able to get free. Of becoming a loner with nothing left but loneliness and contempt for those who won't listen when he wants to explain life."

"The journalist's lot...."

"And what's a waitress's lot? Not getting any tips?"

"Why haven't you put up any Christmas decorations?"

He frowned. "What did you say?"

"Or are you going home to Lund tomorrow?"

"No."

"But your parents—"

"They're both dead. I think so, anyhow."

"You think?"

"Mother and father separated when I was ten. He moved away somewhere...I don't know where. Mother died six years ago. I have only myself. So why the hell should I do anything about Christmas? Christmas comes anyhow."

"Why haven't you got a girl?"

"Oh, lay off now...."

"You're good-looking. You're good in bed, you're—"

"Stop it."

"Don't say you have contact problems," she said with a laugh.

"No."

He cupped his hand over her breast, feeling the nipple stiffen against the palm of his hand.

"I must go home soon."

"I know."

He put his head down on her stomach and let his fingers run through her pubic hair. His tongue sought. Her body rose.

Afterward he lay on his back and she crouched over him and it felt as if he would split apart before he exploded.

"What are you afraid of?" she said sometime later.

He drew in a deep breath, holding it, then breathing out in a long sigh.

"What kind of person is it that takes the same walk night after night, for several years, and yet doesn't seem to exist?"

"What?"

"I'll tell you."

"But he must live somewhere," she said, after listening to his story.

"But where?"

"By the old stadium."

"Look at this...."

He rolled out of bed and walked across the cold floor in his bare feet to his desk. He pulled out the chair and got a pencil and paper. As he drew, she stood leaning over him, one breast pressed against his shoulder.

"It's not much of a map," he said. "But up there by the cross, at the corner of Maria Street and Merchant Street, that's where he stood. That was his goal. He bought a hot dog from Hot Dog Harry. At the snack bar, as it's called, not a hot-dog stall. And if he has a view over the stadium, he must live in one of the two apartment houses I've marked one and two, the only ones on Town Hall Street with a view over the stadium."

"You have a view over the stadium from the apartments on the other side, too," she said.

"You mean along the Avenue?"

"Of course," she said, putting her finger on it. "In the old

days, when there was football in the summer here, and they
played ice hockey in winter, the windows and balconies
were always crowded all along the Avenue. They were the
best places if you wanted a good view over the whole field.
True, it was rather far away from the actual game, but you
saw very well.''

"Saw well?"

"Yes, we often stood there."

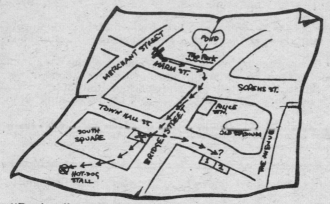

"Don't tell me you live on the Avenue?"

"Yes, didn't you know?"

"No," he said, turning around on the chair and looking at
her. "We know so little about each other."

"Just as well, perhaps. The less one knows, the fewer the
complications. He walked around the block, of course."

"Hell, yes," he said. "It would've been natural to turn
left there at the multicrossroads, walk along Sorens Street
and then turn right down the Avenue. But as his routine included buying a hot dog as the culmination of his walk, he
turned right to get to the square. Instead of going back along
Bridge Street, he continued along Town Hall Street around
the stadium block and onto the Avenue from that direction.
We've got him, I bet you!"

He got up and hugged her.

"We've got him! He must live in one of the apartment
houses there. Where do you live, by the way?"

"On the corner of Sorens Street."

"Then you may even know who he is?"

"What does he look like?"

"Bowed. Bearded. That's about all I know."

"That doesn't say much." She looked thoughtful.

"How many people live on your stairway?"

"Four families."

"No one alone?"

"No."

"Next door, then?"

"No idea."

"Are you going home now?"

"Are you throwing me out?"

"You know I'm not, but you said yourself that you had to be going, and I was just offering to see you home."

She put her forefinger against his nose and laughed. "If it hadn't been for our mystery man, you'd never have offered."

"Don't you be so sure."

"I've been here before, haven't I?"

He smiled guiltily.

BUT THE ENTRANCE DOOR to the three-story house next door was locked, so he couldn't get inside to look at the names on the doors. He calculated that you could also see over the stadium from the apartment house to the right of it.

All the windows were dark.

She wished him a happy Christmas before he went back home.

He walked via the police station and looked inside. There was a light on in there, but otherwise the night was cold and dark. He felt very tired, though filled with enthusiasm for the next day.

THE MAN

THE TELEPHONE RANG the moment he pushed the plug into the socket on the morning of Christmas Eve.

It almost made him leap backward.

"Not first thing in the morning," he muttered half-aloud. He lifted the receiver.

"Hello," he said cautiously.

"Hi! Happy Christmas!"

It was Seved.

"Same to you."

"Has there been something wrong with your telephone? I've been trying to get in touch with you for three hours."

"What's happened?"

"A patrol found another dead dog this morning. They phoned me at half-past five. Where the hell have you been?"

"I unplugged the phone. Do you want me to come down?"

"I'll give you three guesses. And there's a cat, too. How soon can you be here?"

He looked at his watch. Quarter to nine.

"I haven't had breakfast yet," he said. "Be with you in forty-five minutes."

"Okay. Love to Kerstin, and tell her you'll soon be back home again."

"Oh, yes?"

But Seved had hung up before he could ask anything else.

Kerstin was not at all pleased he had to go and the children asked what time Santa Claus would be coming. Not Inger; she said she was too old to believe in Santa Claus. But she was excited all the same.

OSBORN BECKMAN, their technician, had already printed the photographs of the dead dog, and they were now lying in a neat row on the conference table in Olofsson's office.

"You look a wreck," was the first thing Olofsson said. "Have you had a bad night?"

"There's always a lot to do at Christmas," said Holmberg.

"Yes, God knows, there is. We certainly could have done without this. It's not just this animal business. Our friends from Security have been having a shoot-out this morning."

"The terrorist?"

"Who else?"

"So he's here in town after all?"

"Obviously."

"Where did it happen?"

"On Little Cross Street. They were sitting in the car as usual, watching Dack House. The car was on Chestnut Street, so they could keep an eye on the entrance. Suddenly someone came rushing out and started running for dear life along Raby Street, so they got the car started and set off after him. He turned off down Little Cross Street, but as they came around the corner they were shot at and a bullet went right through the windshield. They were bloody lucky. One of them could have bought it. The bullet went slap between them. The driver lost control of the car out of sheer fright, and the car crashed into the fence. The driver got the wheel in his chest and was a bit groggy, but the other man jumped out of the car and started shooting after the runaway. But he just disappeared."

"Disappeared?"

"Yes, the terrorist fired back and the Security guy was forced to throw himself behind the car, and by the time he dared stick his head out again, the man had disappeared. They radioed us, but none of our patrols managed to find a trace of him. We threw a cordon around the area, as far as that was possible with the few night-duty men we've got at our disposal. But he managed to slip through."

"How's the one who got the wheel in his chest?"

"He came to. Slightly hurt, but no broken ribs. They're questioning the girl now. You know, the one who knows Klein."

"What does she say?"

"I don't know yet. They've been questioning her for four hours."

"But how did he get into the building in the first place, past them all?"

"You may well ask."

"God Almighty...."

"And then there's this business of someone not liking our dear dumb friends. At five this morning—about two hours after the shooting—a patrol thought there was something funny about one of the trees outside the station, between the station building itself and the goods warehouse. Outside the taxi station. They found a cat hanging in the tree."

"Hanging?"

"Yes, in a proper noose. According to the vet who looked at it, it wasn't dead when it was hanged."

"Had no one at the taxi station noticed anything? The cat must have howled before being strangled."

"The girl on the exchange, or whatever it's called on the taxi radio, thought she heard something crying out, but couldn't for the life of her think what it was or where the sound came from. The killer must have pulled the cat by its tail to get it to die. The noose was very tight."

"If the noose was drawn tight before it was hung up, that would explain it just as well as pulling on its tail."

"Yes, but according to the vet... well, maybe we'll get some more definite information later. On the other hand we've got a description, if only a rather vague one, of the person who might have done it."

"Where from?"

"A newspaperwoman. Astrid Lindholm was delivering papers in the houses around Clemens Square at the time. She saw a man walking briskly across the square and disappearing along St. Laurence Street. It may not be the animal torturer, but it's something to go on. It was dark, so she didn't see much of him, but he was walking bent forward and he had dark clothes on. She's not sure, but she's almost prepared to swear he had a beard."

"How about the dog?"

Olofsson picked up one of the photographs and held it up.

He looked tired, his pale face against his red beard, dark rings under his eyes. He was wearing a shirt and a knitted cardigan that looked about ten years old and had a hole in one elbow. He had no tie on, and the two top buttons of his shirt were missing.

"You can see for yourself," he said, raising his eyes.

Holmberg studied the photographs in silence, one by one.

It was a golden Labrador. It was lying on its back, its belly slit all the way up to its throat, its legs sticking stiffly out. Its head appeared to be thrown back. The dog was lying in the white snow, the snow all around it red with blood.

"Where was it found?"

"Our poor newspaperwoman again. She was delivering along Charles Street and when she got to one of the entrances she thought she saw something lying in the snow on the other side of the road, behind the fence around the school. When she went and looked through the fence, she saw what it was. After that, she got hold of us.''

"What time did she find the dog?''

"Quarter to six.''

"What time did she see the man?''

"Sometime after five. Quarter past, perhaps.''

"Do we know how long the dog's been dead?''

Olofsson shook his head.

"No, and we don't know whose it is, either. It had no collar on.''

He scratched the back of his neck.

"What a bloody mess this is. What kind of lunatic is around?''

"That's the question. But what about the owner?'' said Olofsson. "Do we try to get something in the papers and ask them to say something on the radio . . . asking the owner of a missing dog to get in touch with us?''

"If the owner hasn't appeared . . . but you'd think the owner would have done that by now.''

Martin put the photographs down and leaned back in his chair. He closed his eyes and turned his face up toward the ceiling. He was tired. He yawned loudly.

"This puts quite a different light on what happened to Bard's dog. It wasn't an isolated attack directed at him or his dog,'' said Olofsson.

Holmberg nodded.

"But the vital question is, why just Bard's dog? It would be altogether too extraordinary if a lunatic just happened to be walking past and took the opportunity just because he happened to have met Queenie. And where did he get hold of the cat and the golden Labrador? He can't have just come across them in town and simply attacked them?''

"You mean there must be a point of contact somewhere, and that it isn't pure chance that Queenie and the golden Labrador and that particular cat happened to fall into his hands?''

Olofsson ran his finger through his thin beard and looked at Holmberg, who again yawned widely. They sat for a long time doing nothing but looking straight at each other.

"I suppose we have to take into consideration that it might happen again,'' said Martin quietly.

Olofsson nodded.

"The worst thing," he said, "is that there's nothing we can do about it. It could happen anytime and anywhere . . . if it happens. And we can't warn people to keep an eye on their animals through the papers, because there aren't any papers over Christmas."

"We've got the radio," said Holmberg.

"Yes."

"That was quite a knife he used to kill Queenie with," Holmberg said suddenly, slapping his thigh as if struck by a thought. "Isn't there anything there we could get our teeth into? Get the vet to do a postmortem on the dog and try to find out what kind of knife it was."

"Perhaps you need a pathologist to do that?"

"I don't think you'll get Fritz doing postmortems on dogs on Christmas Eve," said Holmberg, knowing their clever but crusty police pathologist. "It'll have to be a job for the vet, I should think."

"It's worth trying," said Olofsson. "I'll speak persuasively to Nilsson. I've been in touch with him over this. He's dealing with the Labrador. I'll see if he can form some kind of idea of the weapon. You're right," he said.

"It must have been a very exceptional knife to cut the head off an Alsatian."

Holmberg closed his eyes, trying to imagine how you would attack an Alsatian and kill it without the dog attacking back and biting. He tried to imagine what it would be like slitting open the Labrador without it first scenting danger and counterattacking. How you hanged a cat . . . without it scratching you badly.

"It must be quite a tough guy, too," he said. "I wouldn't even *dare* tackle an Alsatian with intent to injure or kill it. As far as I know, dogs, Alsatians anyhow, are rather sensitive creatures and soon scent danger, and neither are they slow in defending themselves. They do that as soon as they sense the slightest danger."

He shook his head and left the room to go to his own.

If it'd been people, he thought, we'd all have been out in full force.

KERSTIN UNDERSTOOD. She had learned over the years.

"But I hope you'll be home soon," she said. "And the children, too."

"Has anything happened?"

"The telephone rang once, but I was in the bath and

couldn't answer. Inger was out playing with the twins, and
only Anders and I were indoors.''

"What time?"

"About ten."

He looked at his watch. Twenty to eleven.

"Don't answer if it rings again."

"But what if you phone?"

"I'll let it ring three times, then I'll hang up at once and
dial the number again. Then you'll know it's me."

MARTIN HOLMBERG couldn't sit still in his office doing
nothing. He walked all around the building. He went down
to the general office and talked to the duty officer. He took
a few turns outside the door where his colleagues from
Security were questioning the terrorist's girl friend. He
opened the door to Mansson's office, which was empty, and
wondered why Olofsson hadn't called him in

He felt restless, uneasy, nervous. He was smoking too
many cigarettes, chain-smoking so that he lost the taste for
them, but went on just to pass the time.

At twenty-five past eleven an angry and unshaven Mansson appeared.

"Don't you go saying this is a bloody awful Christmas," he
said. "Because you'll be taking the words out of my own
mouth. What have I done to deserve this?"

"The dog murders," said Holmberg.

"I heard something about it."

"Heard *something*? What have *you* heard?"

"I've been busy with the terrorist since four o'clock this
morning. We've been checking all train departures at the
station, and we've had barriers out on all the roads. The
Security boys have managed to get half the force out, and
they've called in their own people from Malmo and even
had some of them flown here on a special plane from Stockholm. Don't you know what's happening?"

"I've enough with the dog killer. Any results yet?"

"What?"

"All those checks and road barriers?"

"No. Not a cat in hell. Either he's managed to give us the
slip or he's still in town. Probably the latter. Hopefully the
former, because then we're rid of the problem. Are they
still questioning her?"

They were standing in the corridor and Mansson glanced
over at the door.

"I should think so. Seems so, anyhow," said Holmberg.

A few minutes later the same door opened and two burly Security men came out with a girl staring defiantly ahead of her. She might have been about twenty-five, hardly more. She was strongly built with thick legs in tight jeans. She had a round face and straggly unwashed hair. She was wearing a grubby blouse.

Five minutes later they returned without the girl.

They knocked on Mansson's door before noticing the piece of paper in the middle of it informing them that Mansson was in the canteen. Holmberg was, too. They were sitting at one of the tables by the windows.

"Jansson," said one of the Security policemen, by way of an introduction.

"Edlund," said the other. "She was a tough nut," he added in his drawling Stockholm accent.

"Have you been questioning her all this time?" said Mansson.

"Yup," said Edlund, tipping his chair.

"All this time," said Jansson. "And she didn't confess to how things were until now, either."

"What had she got to say?" said Holmberg, lighting his fifteenth cigarette that day.

"That the bastard's been living with her all the time," said Jansson.

"But you went there to check," said Mansson.

"Yeah," said Edlund. "But you have to press a button outside the corridor door that rings a bell in the room of the person you want to see," he explained carefully. "And as soon as the bell rang, friend Herbert slipped into the next room. Hers and the other room are slightly apart from the others, but without making an apartment. With a common shower and toilet between with adjacent doors. So he was in there while we were with her."

"We never thought of that," Jansson admitted. "She promised her neighbor she would water her plants over Christmas. That's why she had the key to it."

"But why did he leave today?" said Mansson. "Or last night, I should say?"

"She maintains he couldn't stand being shut in any longer and had to get out," said Jansson.

"But you don't know what to believe," said Edlund. "Could be they're planning some attack over Christmas and he had to go."

"So we've put a special watch on the airport," said Jansson. "And warned the Danes to do the same at Kastrup. The Baader-Meinhof lot have sworn they'll shoot down passenger planes."

He shook his head.

"We'll just have to hope he didn't manage to slip through the net. It'd limit the possibilities a bit if he's holed up here in Lund."

"Yes," said Mansson, getting up. "The possibility of my celebrating a normal Christmas, too. I'm in my office if you want anything."

Holmberg was suddenly left alone with the other two.

Edlund smiled at him.

"And what are you busy doing?" he said in a friendly way.

"Dogs," said Holmberg quietly, also getting up and leaving.

I suppose, he thought, it's possible those two are damned good men, but God help the nation if our security depends on them.

Olofsson was coming toward him.

"Listen to this," he said. "The vet says the weapon must have been some kind of *jungle* knife. That's crazy, isn't it?"

"Don't tell me an Australian aborigine did it," groaned Holmberg, wishing he were home.

His anxiety would not leave him, his anxiety over his family back at home.

I'm supposed to be protecting the general public, he thought. And the general public's pets. But who'll protect my family while I'm doing it?

He wondered if he ought to tell Seved about it, but somehow it seemed slightly embarrassing to mention it.

Probably false professional pride.

18

THE OTHER MAN

Bo Borg had intended to get up early and be off investigating the apartments on the Avenue overlooking the old sports stadium. But he slept late and was woken by the telephone at a quarter to ten.

It was Walter Astrom in a raging fury over his article about the mystery man.

"How did that come about? Who okayed it? *I* didn't."

"No, but head office did."

Astrom took twenty minutes to explain what he felt about that and what his views were. Then he suddenly and unexpectedly calmed down and said it was stupid to quarrel like this on Christmas Eve and the article was well written. Before he hung up, he wished Borg a happy Christmas.

Bo Borg just shook his head.

Werner Soderstrom phoned a few moments later.

Borg told him what he'd found out during the night, though not how he had found it out. At twenty-five past eleven the two of them met where Sorens Street ran into the Avenue.

The stadium fence ran along to the right, apartment houses to the left. The right-hand side was classic territory for anyone who had lived through the memorable ice-hockey matches of the fifties. Sundays during the winter had been synonymous with ice hockey. But the most historic occasion had been a Wednesday, February 16, 1955, the day that had overshadowed all others. That was the day when twelve thousand people from Smaland had invaded Himmelsholm and the stadium to watch the Russians. Seven thousand people did not get tickets and the black-market ticket sellers had fat wallets that day. The Russian players with their enormous caps and almost full-length coats were gaped at from the moment they stepped off the train, like creatures from another planet, supermen, unique, curiosities. They went under the collective name of the Russian

Bears and were considered unbeatable. But a combined
Smaland team had won and a miracle had occurred. Himmelsholm wallowed in the applause. A myth was born.

But the years went by, winters were milder and there
were pleas for an artificial rink. Many people thought
the game a vital advertisement for the town and a team in
the national league self-evident, so development should not
leave the town. And the team, the pride of the town, called
for the best and most modern item of all, an artifical rink.
Fans shouted the loudest, much louder than those who said
what the town and not least young people needed most was
a swimming pool. An artificial rink was built at great expense, and the proud team was soon out of the national
league. Time showed that what was wanted was a swimming pool, so the town got one.

People had jostled on the balconies of the apartment
houses on the other side of the street to watch the game,
the people who lived in them at the time, when Himmelsholm was the ice-hockey mecca of Sweden. Then they were
the most envied people in the town.

Nowadays no one cared who lived there.

"It's not that one," said Borg. "I know that. We'll try the
other two."

"How do you know he doesn't live there?" asked Werner.

"You'll have to take my word for it," said Borg. "Are you
coming?"

They started walking.

It was an absolutely straight road with a gravel surface
and no proper sidewalk, which then ran into Town Hall
Street down by the railway tracks.

The building he didn't live in was white and three-storied,
with a flat roof and icicles hanging from the gutters, apparently knife-sharp and threatening.

They opened the entrance door to the brick three-story
house next door and went into a stairway bathed in daylight
thanks to the large windows on the stairs.

They walked up to the second floor and found two apartment doors, one labeled Bengtsson, the other Ahlsen.

"Well," said Borg, his enthusiasm waning, "what do we
do now? We must ring and ask something, but the worst of it
is we haven't got a decent description of him."

"If anyone in this place has habitually gone out at a certain time night after night," said Werner, "you can be sure
people here know about it."

He rang the Ahlsen's bell, but no one came to the door. On

the other hand, Mrs. Bengtsson was at home. She looked somewhat bewildered.

"Don't you know who you're trying to find?" she said.

She was short, her hair in curlers, her blouse inadequately buttoned, and she was wearing corduroy trousers. She was middle-aged and was holding a lighted cigarette in one hand and an ashtray in the other.

Soderstrom told her. "We simply want to be sure nothing's happened to him," he explained.

She stubbed out her cigarette and put the ashtray down on a small table inside the door.

"I see," she said. But her voice revealed that she had not entirely understood.

"There's no man with a beard living here," she said.

"What about the next block?" said Borg. "The one on the right?"

"I don't really know anyone living there. So I couldn't say anything about that."

"But have you never noticed anyone living there going out night after night?" said Soderstrom.

"No."

That was that. Mrs. Bengtsson was not a person to spend her time at her window finding out what her neighbors were up to.

"Let's try next door," said Borg.

When they came out, they spotted two familiar figures standing on the other side of the road by the stadium fence, looking toward the apartment houses.

Alec Svensen was grinning as he and Barbara Johansson crossed the street.

"I phoned you," said Svensen. "Your wife told me you'd come here. I picked up Barbara on the way. Did you think you could finish this off without us, eh?"

"Have you found him?" said Barbara.

"No," said Bo. "We're just going to try the next block. If he's not there, then I don't know where we look next."

In the next place they were on target first try.

"Yes, that must be Gunnar Palmer," said the landlord. "He lives at the top, on the third floor. He's a bit strange, not peculiar or anything, but reserved and . . . he finds life difficult, seems to shy away from people. He can hardly bring himself to say good morning when you meet him on the stairs. But some people are like that—shy, I mean."

The superintendant's name was Manfred Horn. He was

fifty-five, as thin as a rake and almost completely bald.

"But why are you asking about him? He hasn't done anything, has he?"

"No," said Werner. "We don't think that. But we wondered if anything had happened to him?"

Again he told the story of the man who for years had regularly stood on the same street corner.

"Hmm," said Horn. "Now you come to mention it, I haven't seen him for a week or two. Perhaps he's away for Christmas. I don't see why anything should've happened to him. Have you any reason to think that?"

"Well," said Werner, scratching the back of his neck, "not really. He's always been so punctual, and now that he doesn't come any longer we started wondering."

"What do you know about him?" said Borg.

"Not much. He never causes any trouble. I know he works as a caretaker at Central School. That's about all I know."

"Perhaps we should go up and ring his bell?" said Alec.

But somehow, not one of them wanted to take the first step. They had found his home, and that was good, and they knew who he was, too. But they couldn't very well just go up and ring the bell, could they? When he opened the door—what would they say? How would he react? When all's said and done, his private life had nothing whatsoever to do with them. They couldn't just explain it all by saying that they were wondering why he no longer came. They could always say they had wanted to make sure nothing had happened to him, of course. But what would that sound like?

In some way, it was still an intrusion on his personal life. He might be annoyed and wonder what it had to do with them, and ask what had made them come snooping there.

"What shall we say?" said Barbara. "He might be terribly annoyed."

"But we can't just go away," said Werner. "Can we? We haven't got an answer to our question yet. If he's up there and something has happened to him, and we don't go and find out. . . . I'd never forgive myself if we did nothing."

"You mean he might be lying injured up there?" said Alec.

"He might be dead," said Barbara, in a strange voice.

"We could at least go up and look at the door," said Borg. "If his mail's in the mail slot. . . ."

"But you can't get into his apartment if he's not there," said Horn.

"Then how shall we know if anything's happened to him?" said Barbara.

"I couldn't let you in just like that. What would that look like?"

"But supposing something *has* happened to him?" said Barbara obstinately.

"That's a police matter."

"The police!" snorted Werner. "They don't do anything!"

"How long has he lived here?" said Borg.

"Must be since '72, if I remember rightly," said Horn.

Borg started climbing the stairs. The others stood gazing at his back. Then Soderstrom and Svensen set off after him. Barbara Johansson and the landlord looked at each other.

"What do you want of him?" he said.

"Nothing," she said. "We just want to know why he's stopped going on his walks."

He shook his head.

"It all sounds very peculiar to me," he said. "You lot come raising heaven and earth just because a harmless guy no longer takes his usual walk."

"Does he live alone?"

"Yes. I told you he was a loner. But I've nothing against him, believe you me. He does no harm to anyone. He doesn't disturb anyone and keeps himself to himself. Shall we go up, too, and see what they're up to?"

They caught up with the others outside Palmer's door.

A copy of the *Daily News* was sticking out of the mail slot.

"He hasn't taken in his paper today," said Werner.

"He's probably not at home," said Horn.

"We could ask one of his neighbors," suggested Alec.

"Now listen," protested Horn. "I don't really think I like all this bothering people."

Borg bent down and peered through the mail slot, but all he could see was a bit of the floor and several newspapers lying there. The light was not on inside.

"Have you a key that fits this door?" said Borg.

"Yes," said the superintendent. "But I'm not going to use it."

Borg looked straight at him.

Suddenly he pressed the bell, the shrill ringing echoing in the silence.

Horn stood shifting his feet.

"Perhaps I should phone the police," he said. "Then they can come and send you packing. I have a feeling you're doing something you've no right to do."

"No one can stop us from ringing this bell," said Borg. "It's not *your* apartment block, is it? As far as I know, you're just the super, not the owner."

"I'm responsible for what happens here, and I intend to see that nothing untoward does happen."

"He's not there," said Alec.

"He's probably gone away for Christmas, as I said," said Horn, and they could hear from his voice how angry he was.

His voice was trembling and a high-pitched outburst of fury was imminent.

"I think that's enough now," he said. "Go away! Get out of this house, or I *will* phone the police!"

"Do that," said Borg. "Then they'll have to open up. Ask for Elg and send him our regards."

Horn went rapidly down the stairs, muttering loudly.

A girl opened the door.

Her name was Eva Heed. She was twenty-five and lived alone in this one-room flat, plus kitchen and bathroom, next door to Palmer.

"Gunnar?" she said. "Has he disappeared? Do you think so, too? I haven't seen him for a whole week. I was just wondering what had become of him."

"Do you know him well?" said Borg, suppressing an instinctive desire to put out his hand and touch her hair.

Otherwise it was her eyes that attracted him most of all. They were light and full of a strange luster. Her fair hair framed her face and her lips seemed prone to laughter. Her hair was fluffy, long and very fair. She was tall and slim, with long fingers and beautifully shaped nails, a long neck and a funny way of tossing her head slightly as he looked into her eyes.

"No," she said. "Not well. He's hard to get to know. But he arouses one's maternal instinct; he seems so defenseless, so lonely, but at the same time afraid to do anything about it."

Borg looked at her and nodded.

He was wondering whether they had slept together.

"Do you know if he might be away over Christmas?" he asked.

She shook her head so that her hair swung.

"I shouldn't think so," she said. "He told me once he hadn't any relatives. Anyhow, no close ones. His mother died several years ago. I remember that. He went to her funeral."

"Have you any idea where he might be now?" he said.

"No, but why are you so interested?"

Bo told her.

"He used to go out at night," she said. "I met him sometimes, either on his way out or coming back. We exchanged a few words...ordinary things, you know, about the weather and so on."

A door opened on the landing below and a woman in her outdoor clothes came out with a carry cot in her hands. She put it down while she locked the door. They could see the infant lying on its back staring at the ceiling, well wrapped up under a crocheted cover.

Eva Heed leaned over the railing.

"Hello, Gun," she said. "Have you any idea where Gunnar Palmer's gone?"

Gun looked at her and then at the others.

"Hello," she said. "Yes, he's gone away."

"Gone away?" Werner couldn't help the surprise in his voice, nor the note of disappointment.

"Yes. I met him one day last week on the stairs, and he was on his way down to the car with a suitcase in his hand."

"Did he say where he was going?" said Borg.

"No. He never says much, and I didn't ask. But he went out to the car, put his case inside and drove off."

Barbara laughed.

"That explains everything," she said. "So it wasn't a mystery at all."

"Something mysterious about Gunnar Palmer?" said Gun from below. "I can't believe that. He's the most ordinary person I know."

The air had gone out of the balloon and the explanation of why the man had ceased taking his nightly walks seemed quite natural.

But Stefan Elg did come.

He came up the stairs at a brisk pace with Horn close behind him, Horn's face radiating triumph, malicious triumph.

"Well, here are the police as you requested," he said. "And I got hold of Elg, who said he knew all about you."

"So you found him in the end, did you?" said Elg. "Not bad detective work. Are you quite satisfied now? Or do you still think there's something peculiar about him?"

"He seems to have gone away," said Soderstrom.

"You see, you see! Everything is explained. The super phoned and complained you'd invaded the building and refused to go away unless he unlocked Palmer's door."

"We never said that," said Borg. "Well, that's settled, then. Are you on duty today?"

"I happened to be at the station and they put the call through to me. I thought I might as well nip over. To tell you the truth, I've been curious to know whether you'd track down your mystery man. Now it seems to be settled."

Not one of the four of them had anything to say.

They stood there in silence for quite a long time.

Borg broke the silence.

"Well," he said, putting his hand out to Eva, "thanks for your help. We won't disturb you any longer. Happy Christmas. . . ."

She took his hand and looked at him with a smile that warmed him.

Hell, he thought. If he hadn't gone away, I'd have come back and talked to her, saying I wanted information for an article on the mystery man.

Three minutes later, all five of them were standing outside.

"Well," said Barbara, "I'd better be off home and look after my old man, then, as it's Christmas."

"I'll come with you," said Alec. "Interesting, all this."

Werner was peering at the windows three floors up.

"What are you thinking about?" said Borg.

"I feel empty," he said. "Now . . . now that it's over."

"I think it's a relief," said Alec. "It would have been dreadful if something really had happened."

"But we still have no answer to our question . . . why he stopped coming to stand on that corner every night."

"Now, listen!" said Elg. "Stop making mysteries out of nothing. He took his nightly walk. There's nothing peculiar about that."

Barbara, Werner and Alec slowly started walking home.

Elg and Borg stood looking after them.

"They're disappointed," said Elg. "I suppose they'd at least hoped to find a corpse."

He laughed.

"To tell you the truth, they've made quite a useful contribution. He might well have met with some disaster, been ill and unable to tell anyone or get help. Old people have been found all too often after lying helpless in their apartments until they'd died, just because they hadn't anyone who bothered about them."

Gun came out with her child and stopped by them. She

had flaming red hair and a strong nose, her full lips accentuated by thick lipstick.

She jogged at the baby carriage and also looked up at the window.

"I wonder what happened to his cat," she said.

"Cat?" said Elg.

"Yes, he's got a cat. And he didn't take it with him. But I suppose someone's looking after it. He couldn't have left it on its own in the apartment."

Elg looked at Borg, who had also had the same uneasy thought. Elg decided in the end.

"Come with me," he said to Borg.

He went on ahead through the door and rang Horn's bell, then ordered him to open up Palmer's apartment.

"Now what?" said Horn. "Have you gone stark staring mad? You've just been told he's gone away."

"But his cat?" said Elg. "Where is it?"

Horn hesitated.

"Open up!" said Elg.

"Don't you need permission to do that?" said Horn.

He was not a fanatical law-and-order man, but he thought things should be done properly. He did not wish the slightest complaint to be laid at his door, not least from the owner, to whom he was responsible for the building and its tenants.

"Yes, you do, really," said Elg. "But as a crime may well have been committed, we should take a look."

Muttering, Horn fetched his keys and still muttering, he went on ahead up the stairs. He pushed the key into the lock and turned it.

"I hope we're not exceeding our duties," he said.

Elg shoved him aside and pushed open the door.

The apartment was quite empty. It smelled musty and was dark, as the blinds were all half-down. It was very barely furnished.

There was no rug on the hall floor. A pair of gloves lay on the hat shelf and a pale gray trench coat hung on a peg. The wall was covered with greenish yellow wallpaper.

Along one wall, in the corner, in the only room, was a bed with a bedspread tidily smoothed over it. There was a television set on a low shelf, in the third corner was a low armchair, and beside that a table with an ashtray that needed emptying.

Over by the window was a desk with drawers, a blotter and three ball-point pens in a neat row on top of it. A bookshelf contained a few books and a jumble of papers and magazines. Not a picture on the walls, not a plant on either the table or the windowsill.

There was something totally impersonal about the room. A small table and two chairs stood over by the kitchen window, a dirty glass, a dirty cup and an empty milk carton on the draining board. The refrigerator door was ajar, the refrigerator switched off, inside nothing but a pat of butter, a jar of marmalade and some moldy liver pâté.

A suit, three pairs of trousers and a few shirts were hanging in the wardrobe, a pair of summer shoes, a pair of wooden-soled shoes and a pair of crepe rubber-soled shoes on the floor. There were heaps of cardboard boxes at the back of the wardrobe.

It was Borg who opened the bathroom door and discovered the bathtub was full of water. There was something lying on the bottom.

"Come and look at this," he said.

Elg and Horn came and stood beside him, looking down at the sack that had sunk to the bottom of the tub.

Elg took off his duffel coat and his jacket, rolled up his right shirt sleeve to plunge his hand into the water and take out the sack.

"You could have let the water out," said Borg, pulling at the chain so that the plug came out.

"Hmm," said Elg, glaring at him.

He tried to untie the string around the sack, but it had swollen in the water.

"Is there a knife anywhere?"

Borg found the bread knife in the larder.

Elg put the sack onto the draining board and cut the string.

He opened the sack.

The cat was inside. It had swollen up as a result of being in the water so long.

Horn turned his eyes away and Borg felt the nausea rising.

"Christ Almighty," said Elg. "Christ Almighty. So it isn't that simple, after all."

19

THE MAN

"THEY'VE GONE REALLY CRAZY NOW!" moaned Mansson as he came into Olofsson's room.

Seved and Martin were trying to decide what to do about the animal killer. The question was primarily not actually what they might do about him, because they had not the slightest idea who he was or where they could start looking for him. The fact that the murder weapon was some kind of jungle knife told them nothing. Anyone might own one.

The question was primarily to what extent it would be possible over Christmas to find a team of men ready to tackle the next animal killing, because they had to reckon on the killer's striking again, at least until they had some evidence to the contrary.

The problem was that he might strike again at any time and anywhere. They had no experience to lean on, as this was something quite new.

"It can't be difficult to find cats in town," said Holmberg. "But you don't find dogs alone just anywhere. Hardly any owners let their dogs off the lead. And when they do, they're somewhere around if they're exercising their dogs. Who on earth owned the golden Labrador?"

That was when Mansson came storming in.

"Who's crazy?" said Olofsson.

"Guess."

"What have they done now?" said Holmberg.

"They're thinking of raiding everyone Klein might be hiding with. Together with the Malmo force, they've made up a list of all known left-wing sympathizers, and they've even asked me to make up a list of those we know here. But there are no lefties here at this time of year. Ninety percent of them are students and they've gone home for Christmas to be bourgeois again for a while."

"That doesn't mean Klein hasn't borrowed an apartment or a room," said Holmberg.

Mansson nodded, pressing his lips together.

"Are the roadblocks still up?" said Olofsson.

"Yes, and they're not exactly popular. I'd no idea so many people were out and about on the roads on Christmas Eve. Be grateful you're not involved."

Holmberg got up and went across to the window.

"Don't take it too lightly," he said. "The Security boys may seem a bit farcical, and as if they'd read too many thrillers, but it's no joke for them. They've got an insane terrorist on their hands. The shoot-out last night shows you how serious it is."

"Yes," said Mansson, leaning against the wall. "But Christmas comes but once a year and I'd like to be able to celebrate it."

"You should have thought of that before you became a policeman," said Olofsson.

"Perhaps you'd prefer to join the hunt for the animal terrorist?" said Holmberg. "That's no funnier."

None of them was in a brilliant mood.

"Well, I must go now," said Mansson, adjusting his shoulder holster. "Secret Agent Mansson sets out on another adventure."

"The strange thing is he crossed Clemens Square not so long before the newspaperwoman found the dog, and he had no dog with him then. Where did he find one in such a short time?"

Olofsson picked up a yellow pencil and a note pad. He drew a vertical line down the middle of the paper and began to write.

To the left of the line he wrote, "0500 approx." And to the right of it, "Patrol finds cat acc. P.M. dead for approx. ten minutes. Girl on taxi exchange hears cry sometime between 0445—0455. Cat howling?"

He wrote in the left-hand column, "Approx. 0515." And to the right of the vertical line, "Newsp.-wm sees man walking acr. Clemens Sq."

Then he wrote on the next line, "0545" on the left. And on the right, "Slashed Labrador."

He read what he had written and then pushed the paper across the table and Holmberg picked it up and read it.

"The question really is where he found the dog. And whether he might be living somewhere around there."

"According to a preliminary statement, the dog was killed sometime between five and six. The vet says it's difficult to be more precise than that."

"That's a great help. But why was the dog killed just there? And where did it come from? And why did he first kill the cat and then the dog? Where the hell did he find the dog?"

Olofsson banged his fist on the desk, making the telephone jump, then leaped to his feet so quickly that his chair shot against the wall with a crash.

"I'm going nuts," he said. "Christ Almighty, I'm going nuts! What a bloody awful way of spending Christmas."

"It doesn't make it any better having it rubbed in," muttered Holmberg.

The telephone rang shrilly.

Olofsson grabbed the receiver, listened and then passed it to Holmberg.

"For you."

"Hello," said Martin. "Holmberg here."

"It's me—Kerstin. Can you come home? I'm—I'm getting—getting scared!"

"What's happened now?" he said, half rising.

"I . . . I opened a letter. Addressed to the Holmberg family. There was a card inside it."

He could hear her trying to stop herself crying.

"Steady now," said Martin. "Steady on . . . just tell me what kind of card it was."

"It's a picture—a picture of—of a child. It's—it's a little Jewish child—with his arms in the air and—he's being threatened by a Ger—German Nazi soldier with a g-g-gun. On the back it says . . . ."

He heard her taking a deep breath and swallowing.

"It says, 'Happy Christmas. I shall do to one of your young ones everything you did to me.'"

"God! Listen, go and lock the door. I'm coming back at once."

He threw the receiver down, but it missed and fell to the floor, pulling the whole telephone with it. He rushed over to the door.

"What's up?" cried Olofsson.

"I've got my own terrorist!" shouted Holmberg, jerking the door open.

"What?"

"He's threatening the family now!"

He was through the door.

Olofsson could make neither head nor tail of it.

He looked toward the door, then decided, grabbing his

jacket and then racing after Holmberg. He just had time to leap into the car as Holmberg released the brake and accelerated.

"What the hell's happened?"

He had never seen Martin Holmberg so frightened before, nor so furiously angry.

20

THE SKY IS NEAR

THEN THE SNOW FELL like a thick blanket over Lund, out came the stories of the snowy winters of the Second World War, the winters of '41 and '42 that had become almost legend.

"You should have seen it in those days. The local train to Malmo stuck in drifts on the line . . . once the passengers had to spend the night on the train when the late train got stuck. The snowplow team struggled and shoveled and sweated to clear the line for the train through drifts as high as the steam engines' funnels."

Whenever seventies people remarked on the quantity of snow that had fallen, a forties person would at once raise his voice and explain authoritatively that this was nothing in comparison.

Seventies people listened and nodded and smiled at the old people who had kept those ferocious winters so firmly in their memories. The more they heard, the less they wished to endure such a winter.

It was the afternoon of Christmas Eve and only a few cars were around in town, and one or two pedestrians hurrying on their way somewhere.

The time of joy and fellowship had come.

Candles were lighted and people were friendly and kind to each other. A blue dusk descended and pale stars came out in the endless sky. Human fellowship emanated a warmth like a friendly embrace.

Only the solitary felt the chill silence of a room in which there was no one else.

He experienced the great pain of loneliness at Christmas. It was so quiet then, such embedded quiet.

The other holidays were different. New Year, when people were noisy and there were fireworks everywhere. Easter, with Easter squibs and life filling the hollow of loneliness. The last day of April, when people were out and

about and he could mix in the crowds, an anonymous creature in the anonymous collective, warming himself by the
Walpurgis bonfires. Midsummer, when his yearning for
someone to enjoy the summer's night with him was drowned
by human sounds.

Christmas was the worst, for then he was tormented by
what he did not possess; then his envy of those who had
what had been taken away from him was aroused, and the
hatred of those he blamed for his loneliness swelled.

He was sitting in the armchair staring straight at the wall,
balancing his glass of whiskey on the arm of the chair. The
whiskey tasted of nothing. Nothing tasted of anything,
everything filtering into an external hopelessness. Not
even the instinct to scream out his loneliness was any help
now.

He started, as if waking from a dream. He took a gulp of
whiskey and then put the glass down on the table with a
thump. He rose and went across to the window.

The telephone was on a table in front of the window.

He put his hand on it and seemed to stroke the receiver.

He looked out, unable even to think; the only thing he
could sense was his hatred rising.

He wanted to break something. He wanted to pick something up and hurl it to the ground so that it splintered into a
thousand pieces, at the same time bellowing out his triumph
and ecstasy.

He clenched his fists and swallowed loudly. The pulse in
his temples was beating wildly and he could feel something
gathering into an inner explosion. The need to destroy, to
ruin, to annihilate and obliterate filled him and he found
himself outside his own body, nothing but the tool of this
force, the forces that had taken him over so completely.

He wanted to crush. As they had crushed him.

It was absolutely quiet everywhere now. He looked up at
the sky. The full moon appeared and seemed to grow rapidly toward him, rushing at him like a great glowing globe. He
felt so dizzy, he was forced to lean on the table to stop
himself falling.

It would be dark in a few hours' time, with nothing but the
harsh white moonlight and the acid pricking of the stars.
He would be a minute black spot against all that white on
earth. But nearer to the dark sky, as the darkness of the sky
crept nearer to the earth and pressed him down. Then he
would be forced to heave himself upward, struggling and

striving to stop himself being forced to his knees and unable ever to rise again.

No, he would never be forced to his knees again, never submit to degradation again, never again allow anyone to strip him of his dignity as a human being.

Not that it really made the slightest difference any longer.

But the deathblow in return was a way of making the pain bearable.

His body relaxed and he walked slowly over to the bed, lay down on his back and stared up at the ceiling.

"Happy Christmas," he said quietly.

Then he laughed so quietly, he could hardly hear it himself.

THE PHOTOGRAPH WAS LYING on the coffee table in Holmberg's living room. It was of a boy in a cap and knee stockings, the expression on his face a mixture of fear and total incomprehension of what was happening to him, or why. To the right behind him was a German soldier with a proud expression, apparently posing for the photograph, while in the background Jewish women with bundles, their arms raised, wondering looks in their eyes, were being hustled on by a grim Nazi soldier looking like someone walking home deep in thought.

"What can it mean?" said Holmberg. "What on earth can all this mean? First that Christmas card, or whatever you call it, with a death's-head gnome. Then all that telephoning business. And now this."

"Have you had any dealings with any loonies recently?" said Seved.

"Kerstin said the same thing, but I can't think of anyone. I even called the duty officer to check whether anyone had escaped; no one had. I simply can't fathom what's going on."

Martin ran the tips of his fingers over his eyes, massaging his eyebrows and looking over at the Christmas tree.

The house was totally silent.

The lights on the tree were reflected against the glitter. The Christmas star in the window was lighted, the Christmas toffees hanging on the tree. There was Christmas food in the larder and the refrigerator, and the presents were all waiting down in the basement.

Kerstin and the children had gone to Boel's.

Seved had suggested it and Martin had gratefully accepted. Kerstin had wanted to stay, but had not insisted for the sake of the children, just in case.

They had packed necessities in a case for the night, but they had not taken the Christmas presents with them.

Martin wondered what the children were thinking, how much they understood of why they had suddenly had to leave home on Christmas Eve. What would they think when they didn't get their parcels?

He drew a deep breath and shook his head. "What do we do now? Wait for it to ring and hope for results?"

Seved had contacted the public prosecutor and arranged for the staff at the telephone exchange to try to trace any calls that might come.

"He might be trying different tactics," said Martin. "It's quite a time since he last phoned."

"Think now," said Seved. "Who have you had dealings with lately who might be behind all this?"

Holmberg was tense, sitting there rigidly, his skin apparently stretched over his face, his jaws stiff. The headache was like a band around his forehead and his stomach churned around uneasily. He could have wept.

"There's no one," he said, shaking his head. "There's no one at all."

"Let's go through them," Seved persisted. "You had a battered child case at the beginning of the month, didn't you?"

"Yes, but there was nothing odd about that. She got two months and he was acquitted for lack of evidence. She's still inside and he has no motive. And he wasn't unbalanced."

He shook his head, pressed his lips together and thought about the people he had been in contact with recently, the ones he remembered well.

He couldn't connect any of them with what was happening now. None of them had said, "Wait until this is over, then I'll get you." He was intuitive about that. It always depended on how balanced the person he found himself faced with was. He could read it in their stance, in their manner, their way of looking at him. There was something about every person.

None of those he had been in contact with had emanated a desire for revenge.

During his years as a policeman he had come across people who had eventually been sent to prison. The ones who had taken someone else's life were not what most people considered murderers. They were unhappy people who had killed more or less out of desperation, in many cases trying to draw attention to their own situations, in combination with the desire for revenge.

Then there was the category that mostly in the heat of the battle had struck too hard and killed without meaning to. Tempers rose and the angry blow had landed unexpectedly hard with appalling results.

Then there were the sick, the people with psychic defects. But they weren't usually murderers. For some reason they rarely went that far.

The most dangerous category of all, the most terrifying kind, mostly young people, were those who assaulted their fellow human beings as a matter of course. They were often under the influence of drink or drugs, and then all the inhibitions and barriers were broken down. . .if they had ever been there in the first place. They sought reasons to get involved in disputes.

This most dangerous category was of emotionally disturbed people, emotionally cold at first, and emotionally dead in the final stages. They were the products of a welfare state in which material wealth was the highest aim in life and human relations were frozen and secondary.

Responsible authorities in society tried to explain away the behavior of the violent and vandals by blaming violence on television, in films, in comic-strip magazines and books. Not many people were prepared to admit that violence and vandalism and the lack of humanity and respect for the dignity of human beings were symptoms of something sick in society itself. In the hunt for riches; in unemployment that created boredom and melancholy because of the individual's growing sense of having no place in society; in the destructive environment of concrete suburbs; in the dehumanization of society as a result of the ambitions of decision makers to create an egalitarian society founded on utopian ideals that were sometimes well-meaning but usually painfully impossible to put into practice, because the concept of individuality and the individual had been more or less deliberately forgotten. . . . In this and many other things lay the explanation of why people in this progressive society, when confronted with violence in films or comic strips, found a way of taking revenge on the community that had betrayed them as individuals.

Martin knew that revenge was often involved.

"I honestly don't know who I might have given reason for revenge," he said.

The doorbell rang. Seved went to answer it.

Osborn Beckman was outside, and he was very angry.

"There'll have to be a damned good reason for calling me out on Christmas Eve and leaving the family—"

He fell silent when he saw the expressions on Seved's and Martin's faces.

"Sorry," he said, when Seved had explained. "I didn't know...."

"No, no, but perhaps you wouldn't mind taking this card and examining it to see if there are any fingerprints on it that might tell us something. Mine are on the top right-hand corner. And Kerstin's, because she's handled it. But if there are any more they might be the sender's. See if you can find any."

Osborn nodded.

He straightened his glasses. For once he was not wearing his gray suit, but a dark brown one.

"I'll phone if I find anything. We'll have to reckon with the post-office staff's, too," he said, returning to his car and driving off to the station.

"Oh, well," said Seved, shutting the door behind him. "Now there's nothing to do but wait."

"Terror," said Seved. "According to what I've found out, it's mostly a way for maltreated or at least badly treated and misused people of saying how bloody awful life is for them, drawing the attention of the world to their problems. It's a desperate cry for help."

"So you mean that this may not be directed at me personally, but that I've been picked out by a madman as a symbol or representative of something that caused or is still causing the man's bloody awful state?"

"I don't know."

"At the moment I have no sympathy whatsoever with such cries for help, whoever's making them. I want to get the swine!"

Seved nodded.

"You see what I mean?"

"No," said Holmberg. "At the moment I don't want to see anything."

The telephone rang.

"Can't be Osborn already," said Seved.

"Shall *I* answer?"

Olofsson nodded.

Holmberg lifted the receiver.

"Hello."

Nothing happened.

"Hello!" he shouted. "Wouldn't it be a good thing if we met and talked this out instead of going on with this lunacy? What the hell do you want? Say something!"

He heard a click and then the dial tone again.

A minute or so later they were informed by the exchange that the conversation had been too short for them to trace the caller.

A moment or two later it rang again.

This time it was the duty officer from the order police, who informed them that another animal had fallen victim to the unknown Jack the Dog Ripper, as one of them had now christened him.

BO BORG WAS SITTING on the sofa at Elg's place, drinking mulled wine. Stefen had not been able to resist the impulse to invite him back to Christmas dinner.

They had searched Palmer's apartment to try to find something that would explain his disappearance. They had spoken to other people in the building to try to form some idea of the man or some explanation for why he should drown his cat and disappear.

Elg had been struck instinctively by the thought that Palmer had gone away somewhere to take his own life.

The only item their conversations with the other people in the building had produced was a reasonable description of the man's appearance: medium height, middling fair hair, beard, no distinguishing marks.

But no one had been able to tell them anything about the man called Palmer. He had been a stranger living among them, someone who never made a disturbance, a shadowy figure living his own life and creeping around never letting anyone else near him.

His apartment had been astonishingly and frighteningly sterile, in that everything that gives a human being personality and profile in the form of possessions and souvenirs had been totally absent. Not a single photograph, framed or unframed; not even a photograph album. No private letters, only bills neatly kept in a ring file. The only personal objects they found were a bundle of notebooks in the bottom drawer of the desk, and that drawer had been locked. Borg had prized it open with the aid of a knife.

Both Borg and Elg had leafed through the notebooks.

They seemed to be full of apparently meaningless notes, the product of the chaos of a confused mind more than anything else. Notes on everything between heaven and earth, on the mechanism of loneliness, on hatred, on survival in a world of dead men, on everything imaginable, but all of it theoretical and abstract.

"A veritable madman," Borg had said, reading aloud a piece headed, "A Modest Suggestion on How to Save the Swedish Economy."

Palmer suggested that everyone should stop working and that New Day's Eve should be celebrated three hundred and sixty-four days a year. New Year's Eve should be done away with, and instead everyone should celebrate New Day's Eve. Every midnight should be celebrated with drinks and the letting off of magnificent fireworks.

A certain amount of time would have to pass before this measure would have the desired effect, but if rumor of these new Swedish customs spread all over the world and people from other countries came as tourists to experience and study these peculiar northern Europeans, who:

. . . like the human race, in desperation in face of the final catastrophic end of the world, wished to enjoy at any price every moment, knowing full well that at any moment the world and mankind would come to an end and that waiting for New Year's Eve was all too difficult.

But it must seem clear what a gigantic economic advantage this monstrous invasion of tourists would bring to the sorely tried national treasury, and how trade and the tourist industry would flourish at all levels.

I see as in a vision the poorest people in the underdeveloped countries pawning their last grain of wheat to provide the means to purchase the fare to this remarkable country of strange people.

Sweden would become the center of the world. But New Year's Eve would be abolished, for not many tourists could possibly be expected then, as they would probably prefer to celebrate the New Year in their own countries. Gradually, it could be calculated that other countries would take to celebrating the New Day with the intention of increasing both the country's and the inhabitants' wealth thanks to the tourist industry. But it would soon be clear that in the end no one would be left to act as tourists.

This might well save the Swedish economy, but in the long run it would actually be no more than a step on the way to a definitive degeneration and destruction of the human race.

I see before me the peoples of the earth clinging in desperation to life and extracting the last possible drop out of each day. There is going to be one single gigantic dance of death, camouflaged by excesses of celebration, feasting, binging, gorging, copulating, drinking and torrents of joy, all to the notes of blaring music and the crackling of fireworks.

"There's some method in his madness, anyhow," said Elg. "He must be desperate."

Elg had spoken on the telephone to the headmaster of the Central School to find out about his caretaker.

He had been told than Gunnar Palmer had worked there since the autumn term of '72, that he had moved from Lund to Himmelsholm, and that he had been found guilty of a driving offense in Lund.

What sort of driving offense?

The headmaster could not remember.

Neither could he understand why he was being disturbed in the middle of Christmas Eve and asked about Palmer.

"He has disappeared."

"Palmer? That's hard to believe. My impression of the man is entirely positive. He's reliable and conscientious. He's quiet and orderly, and has never done anything offensive, but has carried out his work in an exemplary manner. What has he done?"

"Nothing as far as I know. I told you he seems to have disappeared."

"Extraordinary."

"He's drowned his cat."

There had been a long silence at the other end of the line.

"He's done *what*, did you say?"

"Drowned his cat."

"Extraordinary."

"Maybe so. Do you know whether he was friendly with anyone at the school? Anyone who might know something about him? Had he any personal friends?"

"All friends are personal, aren't they? I haven't any other kind."

"Hmm."

"No, I don't know anything about him, apart from what I've told you. As far as I know, no one in the school was close to him. It's not usual for teachers and caretakers to be friends. If you don't mind, I'd really rather like to return to my family now."

So the headmaster had hung up.

"You could phone the police in Lund," Borg had suggested. "About that driving offense."

"Do you think anyone would remember after all these years?"

"You could try, anyhow."

"Yes, as he came from Lund, of course I must. I'll have to alert them if we're going to work together, should he appear there, and I must send out a general description. I can do that. Then I'm going home to Saga and the kids. It *is* Christmas, after all."

So now Borg was at home with them.

He had not really wanted to intrude, but Elg had insisted.

"Saga will be delighted if you come," he had said.

And she had been.

So had the children, their daughters, Malin and Lotta, four and two years old, inquisitive, questioning, lively.

Borg basked in the warmth of their home, trying to envelop and curl himself up inside it.

"There we are, then," said Elg. "They've promised in Lund to let me know if they find anyone who knows Palmer. Perhaps we'll get some hint of what he might have been up to. Looking for anyone over Christmas is hopeless. What do you like to drink with your meal? Vodka?"

"Please."

"How nice you could come," said Saga as they sat down at the table.

"JUST AS WELL YOU CAME," said Fransson.

He and Rosen were the first two policemen on the spot. It was a quarter past five and the dead dog was lying just inside the entrance to a multioccupied block in North Vall Street, a small cul-de-sac to the right off Broad Street, parallel to All Saints Church.

A dachshund. Its head had been cut off.

A broad-shouldered man was standing beside it impatiently shuffling his feet with suppressed rage.

"As I told him there," he said, pointing to Fransson, "it's the bloody limit you can't stop this kind of thing. If I'd been a bit quicker and those dumb flatfoots hadn't stopped me, I would have nabbed him by now, and *he*'d have been dead."

"Who are you and what are you talking about?" said Olofsson sharply.

"Who am I? Nilsson, of course."

"Are you the owner of the dog?"

"Yes, I damned well am."

"Calm down a bit and tell us what's happened," said Olofsson.

"Calm down! When dumb slobs like that interfere and stop a man doing something about things like this—" he said, pointing at the dachshund.

He was scarlet in the face, his hair sticking out in all directions.

"We took this away from him," Fransson explained, holding out an ax.

"Will someone please tell me what has happened," said Olofsson patiently, with a note of authority to bring the situation back under control.

"We were driving down Broad Street," said Fransson. "And we saw two men running, tearing straight across the road. We nearly ran over the first one. Behind him came Mr. Nilsson here, wielding that ax. Naturally, we leaped out of the car and caught and disarmed him. By the time we'd managed to do that, the other man had vanished."

Olofsson nodded.

"They almost twisted my arms off!" shouted Nilsson. "Wouldn't it have been more sensible to have tried to catch the person who cut my dachshund's head off?"

Holmberg squatted down beside the dog and looked at the cut. The head lay several feet away from the body, over by the wall where it had rolled, a trail of blood between head and body.

He looked at the headless body for so long that he began to feel sick and had to get up and look away.

"May we hear what happened?" said Olofsson.

"I was going to walk the dog," said Nilsson. "When I got down here—I live three floors up—I found I'd forgotten my matches in the apartment, so I went back up to fetch them, leaving the dog down here. I went back up, put the key in the door, and then he started barking. I went in and when I was in the kitchen to get the box of matches—they were on the kitchen table—I heard a sort of howl and then it was suddenly stopped. I rushed out and down the stairs."

"What did you think had happened?"

"How the hell would I know? But I realized something was wrong. He could have got entangled in his lead and been strangling himself. When I got halfway down the last flight I saw what had happened. And I saw the person who did it, too."

"Can you describe him?"

"I bloody well can! I know who it is."

Olofsson started involuntarily and Holmberg dropped his packet of cigarettes out of sheer surprise.

"Who?"

"Sture Kvist. He lives over on Peace Street. He's got a daughter living in this building."

It sounded too good to be true.

"How do you happen to know him?" said Holmberg.

"How do I . . .?" said Nilsson in surprise. "Because we're workmates, that's how! The bloody swine! Just wait till I get my hands on him!"

"Now, now," said Olofsson. "Just tell me the facts. What happened? How was he standing when you saw him, and what was he doing?"

"He was leaning over the dog, and then he turned toward me and I shouted at him, 'What the hell are you doing?' He just looked surprised and scared. He said nothing, but just sort of gasped. I turned and rushed back upstairs and got the ax from just inside the door."

"Why do you keep an ax just inside the door?" asked Holmberg.

"I don't keep an ax just inside the door! It happened to be standing there. I'd used it for putting the Christmas tree into the base. So I grabbed it, thinking I'd bloody well give him it now, and rushed downstairs again. And would you believe it, the swine was on his way upstairs! When he saw me with the ax, he spun around and set off like greased lightning with his tail between his legs. If it hadn't been for those two dumb oxen, I'd have caught up with him and cut his own bloody head off."

Olofsson looked at Fransson, who shrugged.

He looked up the stairway, wondering why no curious crowd had collected.

"Isn't anyone at home here?" he said.

"No," said Nilsson. "Only my wife. Though she's not at home, either. She's working over Christmas. She's a nurse. All the rest have gone away and some are probably at church."

"Isn't Kvist's daughter at home, either?"

"No, she and her husband have gone to Majorca for Christmas. They went yesterday. Are you going to stand here all night? Aren't you going to go and get him?"

Holmberg looked at the man.

"Were you really going to cut his head off?" he said quietly.

Nilsson spun around.

"Didn't he cut Lester's head off?"

"Lester . . . is that the dog's name?"

"Yes. Anything wrong with that?"

"No, no. Do you normally get on with Kvist, or aren't you friends for some reason?"

"We've never been what you might call friends. The swine has been to my place, and we've had a drink together, and we've always got on all right. I don't understand—I don't understand how he could—"

He drew a deep breath.

"He must be off his head," he said with conviction and some heat. "People like that should be locked up. And to think I've been mixing with someone like that, and working with him."

"Where do you work?" said Holmberg.

"I drive a bus."

"We're going over to Kvist's place now," said Olofsson.

"I'm coming with you."

"No, you're not. Go on upstairs and wait for us. Until we come back. I understand exactly how you feel, and you're upset, but—"

"I'm not upset. I could kill him! Doing such a thing to an innocent animal! Lester had never done him any harm!"

"Now please go on up and wait for us at your place," said Olofsson.

He looked down at the decapitated dog.

"Have we got anything to put him in?" he said to Rosen.

"We've got some plastic bags in the trunk."

Olofsson nodded.

Ten minutes later they parked the car outside the apartment house on Peace Street.

It was a short street between Spool Street and Charles XII Street, lined with tall buildings from about the turn of the century.

They had reinforcements in the form of four patrol cars, so in all they were now two plain-clothes and eight uniformed men.

They looked up the facade toward Kvist's window and saw two faces, a man's and a woman's. The faces vanished rapidly.

The police went in through the entrance. Seved and Martin went up the stairs first, closely followed by two uniformed men with their guns drawn.

They heard steps coming down and when they got to the second floor they were met by a man who looked quite terrified, to say the least of it.

"What do you want?" he said in a low voice. "I haven't done anything. Was it Oswald who put you on to me?"

"Are you Sture Kvist?"

"Yes."

He was about fifty and balding. He was wearing a gray cardigan and brown trousers. He was very thin and quite short, rather like a carelessly cut stump of rope. He was trembling all over.

"He seems to think I killed his dog. He's mad! I thought he was going to kill me with his ax! He would have done if those policemen hadn't appeared and stopped him. He can run much faster than I can. How could he do such a thing? Trying to kill me with an ax. I'm scared silly. I mean, first I almost fell over that poor dog, and then he came at me with an ax! Did he do it? Did he cut the head off his own dog? He must have gone mad."

An equally short but much plumper woman came slowly down the stairs.

"Have you got him?" she said. "He tried to kill Sture!"

"He got it in his head that you had killed his dog," Holmberg said.

"He must be crazy," said Kvist. "As if I would...."

His voice failed him and he was forced to sit down. "It must have been that other man! The one who nearly knocked me over when I came out of the entrance door. It must have been him!"

"Who?"

"Sture only went over to Mary's to see that her apartment was all right," his wife said. "We promised our daughter we'd keep an eye on it while they were away."

Kvist raised his head.

"I went for a walk after dinner and thought I'd just pop up and see everything was all right. There are so many break-ins."

"What happened when you went in?"

"Well, I opened the main door and *vroom*! Before I could blink, a man came at me and almost knocked me over, and then off he went up the street. And when I was on my feet again I saw the dog lying there. Then Oswald appeared and—well, you know the rest."

"Why didn't you explain to him what had happened?"

"I wasn't given a chance! He rushed back up and when I went to see if there was anything I could do—I was going to tell him about the man who'd shot out like a bullet from a gun—he just bawled and threatened me with that ax. I just ran as fast as I could back home. If those two policemen hadn't appeared, I don't think I'd ever have seen my own home again."

He was trembling and shaking and looking rather sick.

"Can you describe him?" said Olofsson.

"It was all so quick. But he had a thick coat on, one of those military coats or whatever you call them. And army boots. And he was bareheaded."

"Had he got a beard?"

"No, I don't think so. But his hair was long. And he was big and strong. He was holding one hand inside his coat and it wasn't buttoned up. Yes, he did have a beard, I think. One of those short ones. Like a skipper's beard. Now I come to think of it, I remember it quite well."

He closed his eyes and clasped his stomach.

"I'm not feeling very well," he said.

"Did you recognize him at all?" said Holmberg.

"No, never seen him before. What kind of maniac does that sort of thing? I heard about the dog they found in the park quite near here. Walde's dog. It had been ripped open. It's horrible, that's what it—"

"Walde? Which Walde?"

"The Walde girl across the road."

"Does she own a golden Labrador?"

"Yes, she does."

"But why on earth hasn't she reported that the dog is hers?" said Olofsson.

"Hasn't she?" said Kvist in surprise.

"I don't think she's at home," said Kvist's wife. "Her apartment is quite dark. I noticed that before."

"But she can't have left the dog alone at home?" said Holmberg.

"Oh, no. There was a light on there this morning, because I saw it when I let the kitchen blinds up after breakfast."

"What do you know about Miss Walde?"

"Nothing. Just that she lives there. The fact is, I didn't even know her name until Mrs. Gustafsson told me Miss Walde's dog had been found dead and battered."

She shuddered.

"Which floor does she live on?"

But they could see for themselves that her apartment was dark when they looked up at the window on the third floor. Neither did they get any response when they rang the doorbell.

They were just trying to decide whether to get a search warrant or not when the police radio called them up.

Holmberg was told that someone had thrown a stone through the kitchen window of his house.

They had posted Martinsson inside the house, so that it wouldn't be left empty while they were away. He reported that there had been no more telephone calls, but there had been a stone.

"I've put a piece of cardboard over the window," Martinsson said. "I found one in the basement. Nothing damaged in the kitchen, except the window."

"Thanks."

"I went out to ask your neighbors whether any of them had noticed anything, but it's dark in practically every house here. There seems to be no one at home at all in your terrace."

"No, it's usually like that over the holidays. Listen. . .I'll be back as soon as I can."

"Okay."

Two messages came over the police radio.

The police in Himmelsholm had been inquiring about a man by the name of Gunnar Palmer.

An infant had been found in the backseat of an abandoned car outside Central Station.

21

UNTO US A CHILD
IS GIVEN

THE SCREAMS HAD DRAWN ATTENTION to it. A station employee
on his way home had heard screams from a Volkswagen car
parked outside the main station building. He had gone
across to the car and seen the child in the back. He had tried
to open the door, but the car had been locked. So he'd run
back into the station and phoned the police. But a woman
had already alerted them anonymously. Olofsson and Holmberg in one car and four patrol cars containing eight
uniformed men all drove there.

The Volkswagen was parked along the curb by the newspaper kiosk, slap opposite Central Station. It was the only
car on the whole street.

The screams penetrated out to them, as if the car were
vibrating and shaking from them.

The station man was looking irresolute.

"Perhaps we could smash a window?" he suggested.

Fransson bent his arm and drove his elbow at the right-
hand front window. It held. He took out his gun and struck
with all his strength at the glass. The window split with a
loud crack and Fransson thrust his hand inside to open the
door.

He put down the front seat and leaned inside to lift the
child out of the carry cot. Its screams were piercing.

The child was enveloped in a thick rug and had a coverall
and a cap on. It was warm and sweaty from all that screaming in the cold car.

"There, there," said Fransson, pressing the child to him
and rocking it on his arm until slowly the screams subsided
and the child started hiccuping.

Fransson was thirty-eight and had a twelve-year-old son.
He reckoned the child was about two. Fransson was tall and
dark, his oval face covered with acne scars, and he had a
small mustache below his straight nose.

The child pressed against him and put its head down on his shoulder, drawing a deep breath that sounded like an explosive sigh. Then a shudder went through the small body and suddenly the child fell asleep.

"Wonder how long he's been there?" said Olofsson. "Or she."

"Looks like a girl," said Holmberg.

"Myrtle Walde," said Rosen, getting out of the car. "It says on the owner's plaque."

"What the hell?" said Olofsson. "What the hell's going on?"

"What shall we do with the child?" said Fransson. "Take it back to the police station? It needs changing."

"I don't think there are any diapers at the police station," said Olofsson, his thoughts elsewhere. "We'd better leave her at the Children's Clinic. She can stay there until we trace the mother, or find out what's happened to her. Could she have parked the car here? First the dog. . . and now the child. Fransson, you take her up to the Children's Clinic."

"Rosen can drive. I can't hold her and the wheel at the same time."

"Okay. We'll go back to Peace Street. We must get into Walde's apartment."

"Do you mind if I go down to the station?" said Holmberg.

"What for?"

"I want to phone the police in Himmelsholm."

"Why?"

"This Gunnar Palmer. . . do you remember him?"

Olofsson looked blank at first, but then he began to remember. His eyes grew distant and he nodded.

"You do that," he said. "The rest of us'll go to Myrtle's place. Tell me, do you think Palmer and what's been happening at your place might be connected?"

Holmberg flung out his arms.

"Do you remember him?" he said.

"I remember him. I find it hard to believe."

"So do I. But I remember him once saying during interrogation that he was finished as a human being. It'd be . . . ."

He took the car, and Olofsson got a lift in one of the patrol cars.

ROSEN BRAKED AND STOPPED outside the low building along Geting Road with a piece of sculpture outside it. The Children's Clinic had been built in '51 and was in the shape of an H, the left-hand wing a two-story building with its facade facing Geting Road. The piece of sculpture was called *Mother*, the work of Carl Eldh, and it had been unveiled in January '57.

"You wait here," said Fransson. "I'll be back in a minute."

He went in through the glass doors, turned right, opened a door and found himself in a corridor stretching coldly and emptily away. He walked slowly along it looking into the rooms, the sleeping child against his shoulder.

He saw a nurse putting a bandage on a boy's hand under the anxious scrutiny of his parents.

She looked up. "Hello," she said. "What've you got there?"

"Lost child, so to speak. Will you be free soon?"

"Yes, soon. Could you go and wait in the next room?"

He did so.

He sat down on a chair and put the little girl down so that she was resting along his legs. She opened her eyes, looked uneasily and quickly at him, then smiled and fell asleep again.

He undid the ribbon of her cap and carefully eased it off. She had fair hair, thick and long. He pulled down the zipper of her coverall and eased that off her. She half looked at him but went on sleeping, smiling slightly. She was wearing a yellow sweater and a pair of trousers. Her bottom was very wet and it was clear she had not been changed for a long time. She was warm all over because she had been lying well covered by the rug, and also because she had been screaming for so long.

He put her down on a bunk to change her soaking diaper.

She woke up properly and started saying words he could not understand. She couldn't be two, he thought.

He suddenly noticed the nurse standing in the doorway.

"You seem to be making yourself at home," she said. "What's wrong with her? She's not been battered, has she?"

"I don't know if anything's wrong with her. We found her abandoned in the mother's car, and we've no idea where the mother is."

"But you can't leave her here just like that."

"But what shall I do with her?"

"Social Services."

"On Christmas Eve? Happy Christmas, by the way."

"Same to you. What's it like working at Christmas?"

"I finish at eight o'clock. What's it like for you?"

"I'm used to it. This is my third year running. But just you wait till next year."

"Can you give her some food and put her to bed?"

"What's her name?"

"No idea. Yes, her surname's Walde."

The child never took her eyes off him. She was lying on her back, kicking her legs in the air, so the blanket fell to the floor.

"Okay," he said. "Look after her, won't you?"

"You're sure there's nothing wrong with her?"

"There doesn't seem to be. She was well wrapped up and tucked in, so she hasn't been cold. But she's bound to be hungry."

"How long had she been alone in the car?"

"No idea. But she was exhausted from crying when we found her."

He went over to the bunk and stroked the child's cheek with his finger. Then he nodded to the nurse and went out of the room. He had taken no more than two steps when he heard the howl and following storm of tears. He walked on, but she howled even louder, almost completely drowning the nurse's comforting words. He slowed down and with his hand on the door handle stopped and listened. The child's screams penetrated down the corridor.

He turned slowly around, then went back.

The girl was struggling to get out of the nurse's arms. He stood irresolutely in the doorway, then both nurse and child became aware of his presence. The child opened her eyes and saw him. With a shriek she stretched out her arms toward him.

He went in and took her. She stopped screaming and clung to him, her tears gradually subsiding into sniffing and hiccuping.

"Perhaps I oughtn't to have come back?" he said.

"It'll be more difficult to get her to calm down when you go now," she said.

"Listen, now, young lady. You have to stay here. This lady will give you something nice to eat, and then you can go to sleep in a nice bed. That'll be good, won't it? Sleep well."

He tried to loosen the grip of the small hands from his shoulder strap, and when he was finally successful he held her out to the nurse.

The child immediately started screaming and kicking,

almost hurling herself into the air and twisting around. He held her to him again and she calmed down.

"Listen, little miss, you have to stay here. We'll find your mama, you'll see."

"Dada," said the child, leaning her head on his shoulder.

"Oh, Lord!" said Fransson. "I should have kept going through the door. But I never used to be able to stand it when my own boy screamed when he was little. I've never been able to stand hearing children crying. Makes me ill. Hurts in some way. What do we do now?"

"Well, either you'll have to stay until she falls asleep, or you'll have to endure her screaming the place down when you go."

"I can't do that. I'd hear her screams all over Christmas. Where will she be sleeping?"

"Food first. Follow me."

They met Rosen in the corridor.

"You're taking a hell of a long time. Does it take all that time to hand over a kid?"

"You can wait in the car. I'll come as soon as I can."

"How long will you be?"

"An hour at the most."

"An hour! You're crazy. What the hell's up with you? Is the kid ill or something?"

"Something."

"But they've got doctors here who can look after her, haven't they? You're a nurse, aren't you? You can see to her, can't you? We've got other things to do."

"Wait in the car."

Stig Rosen was fifty-five years old and unmarried. He had large hands with thick fingers, and his experience of kids consisted of his efforts to train a passable junior handball team. He was conservative, to put it mildly, a voluble monarchist, and was considered by many people to be insensitive and somewhat sluggish.

"What the hell are you up to?" he said.

"Doing my job," said John Fransson, walking away with the child in his arms and the nurse behind him.

She was twenty-seven, red haired, and according to the badge on her chest her name was Gunnel Dennison.

Rosen watched them go, shaking his head and slapping his cap against the wall, muttering.

AFTER A GREAT MANY ifs and buts, Olofsson managed to make contact with the apartment manager's substitute, as the manager himself was away for Christmas. It took some time to persuade him that he could unlock the door of Myrtle Walde's apartment without risking being charged or any other unpleasant consequences. Olofsson had just gone through the door when Mansson and Westerberg turned up.

Westerberg was on duty and Mansson appeared to be in a good mood.

"I'm on my way home," he said. "The Security boys have finished. They've heard that Klein has been positively identified as one of the passengers on a ferryboat between Rodby and Puttgarten. So the Danes and the Germans can take over now."

"That's good news. So now you're free and can go home?"

"Yes indeed. Home for Christmas. That's it."

"Don't forget you're on call."

"No, I won't."

"Good. Then you'd better stay now."

Mansson gave vent to his fury to such a degree that Olofsson gaped and Westerberg chuckled beneath his thin mustache.

When Olofsson had explained, he calmed down, but pointed out that he was very tired.

"Who isn't?" muttered Seved. "Let's see what we can find from this apartment now."

It was a two-rooms-plus-kitchen apartment, large rooms with high ceilings and handsome windows. The bed in the bedroom indicated that the occupant lived alone. A single parent. There was a cot against the bedroom wall with a baby table beside it. The bedroom smelled unpleasant and they traced the smell to a bucket of soaking diapers with the lid on.

Both the cot and bed were unmade. A drawer in which Myrtle kept her underclothes was pulled out and the wardrobe door was open. Some of the clothes had fallen off their hangers.

There were dirty dishes in the kitchen, apparently from several days' meals, and all the ashtrays in the apartment were filled to the brim with butts of cigarettes with no filters.

The apartment gave the impression of having been left in a hurry, but they could find nothing to explain why.

"Could it have been the mother who phoned us anonymously?" suggested Westerberg.

"What the hell was she afraid of, and in that case, what has she fled from?" said Olofsson. "What do you know about her?" he asked the temporary manager, who lived on the floor above.

"Not much. She works at the post office and has always been quiet and well behaved. No wild parties, and no men in and out. But I don't know much more."

"You haven't heard anything special these last few days?"

"No. What might that be?"

"Her dog?"

"Yes, that was peculiar," said the man. "The dog barked like mad this morning, and doors were slamming somewhere, and I heard someone shriek, but that's all."

"Were you asleep and woken by the noise?"

"Yes."

"Did you get up and look to see what it was about?"

"No."

Olofsson looked at him.

"Why not?"

"Well...it stopped."

"But weren't you curious?"

"Well...."

"Wouldn't it have been natural to find out what had happened?"

"Yes, perhaps so. But my wife told me to stay and not go out onto the stairway. She didn't want me to get involved in anything. The Altwalls next door sometimes quarrel rather loudly, so I assumed it was them again. And that the dog had been woken by it and was barking as a result."

"At that hour of the morning? Do they usually quarrel at that time?"

"I don't know about that."

"You didn't by any chance hear a child crying, as well, did you?" said Mansson.

"Yes, but I just thought the kid had been woken up by the noise. Why do you ask?"

"I just wondered."

"We ought to ask around to find out how many people heard anything," said Westerberg.

"Not many people are at home. Most of them have gone away for Christmas."

"That's something that always surprises me," said Mansson. "A hell of a lot of people go away for Christmas. Where do they all go? And why don't people come here?"

"You may well ask," said the manager, flinging out his arms.

They found Mia and Tore Altwall. They'd heard Myrtle Walde's doorbell ringing sometime between five and half past in the morning.

They'd heard the dog barking and the child crying and Myrtle saying, "Go away. Leave us alone."

They had heard the dog yelping and suddenly stop, then the sound of quick but heavy footsteps going down the stairs and finally the entrance door closing.

"Someone trying to get at her," said Mansson. "And then she set the dog on him. Must be Jack the Dog Ripper."

"*Who* did you say?" said Holmberg.

"That's what they call him down at the station."

"Oh, I see. Amazingly witty."

"But why did he attack Bard's dog and the dachshund? Why did he hang the cat? If he was out to get her?"

Olofsson went over to the window and looked out.

"I've never heard anything like it," he said. "I thought people were inquisitive. In my experience, they are. But not a soul in this building got out of bed, or even looked out of the window to see if they could see anything. It's one thing not opening your door, quite another not even looking out of the window."

"People *are* inquisitive," said Westerberg. "But they're scared when frightening things happen near them."

Westerberg was philosophically inclined.

The explanation of why no one had looked out of the window was that no one had wanted to get involved. And then it had gone quiet again.

"It must've been some man getting in a rage with her for some reason," said Mansson. "The point is, what on earth do we do on a night like this to find out about the men in Myrtle Walde's life?"

"There's a black address book on the telephone shelf in the hall," said Mansson. "We could phone around the people in it."

Olofsson got it and leafed through.

"It's not exactly crammed full," he said. "This would take some time all the same. But I suppose we'd better do it. I wonder if he's in here?"

They armed themselves with as many photographs of Myrtle Walde as they could find before leaving for the police station.

There was a whole box of photographs. In most of them she was dressed, and her pose and clothes pointed to the fact that she was a model, perhaps for fashion advertisements or a clothing catalog. In some of the pictures she was more skimpily clad or else had no clothes on whatsoever.

They took the whole box with them.

The nude photographs were like those found in what are called men's girlie magazines.

Myrtle Walde was a genuine blonde. She had long fluffy hair and a slim, well-developed body. Her breasts were large and she appeared to be sunburned all over, a factor explained by the quartz lamp at the back of the wardrobe.

She was a very pretty woman, very attractive, with an open, intelligent face.

"Perhaps we'd better not distribute the nude pictures to the boys who've got to look for her," said Mansson.

"No, you keep them, you dirty old man," said Westerberg.

ON HIS WAY INTO the police station, Holmberg met Osborn Beckman on his way out.

"Hi," said Beckman. "I phoned you at home, but you weren't there. I asked Martinsson to tell you about those fingerprints."

"Did you find any?" said Holmberg.

"Yes. There were some from someone you perhaps remember."

"Gunnar Palmer?"

Beckman looked surprised.

"How did you know?" he said.

"I just know," said Martin.

"The hell you do! Here's me, dragged away from home on Christmas Eve to help out, and after hours of work and one hell of a day getting that information out of the register and finding you to tell you, and you tell me you already *know*! Christ Almighty! What was the point, if you already knew?"

"I've only just found out."

"Huh!" exclaimed Beckman, stomping off toward his car.

Martin watched him go.

"Happy Christmas," he said quietly.

He hurried inside and sat down at his desk.

He hadn't switched the light on. He sat gazing out into the darkness, absentmindedly lighting a cigarette.

He inhaled deeply and cleared his throat.

He was feeling very tired and utterly shattered, as if the air had gone out of something, now that he knew who it was.

Before, as long as the threat had been nothing but an unknown shadow, it had seemed horrible. Now he knew . . . it was no longer horrible now that he could attribute it to a human being.

He couldn't be absolutely sure it was Palmer just because he had heard the police in Himmelsholm wanted information about him. But as soon as he had heard, something had clicked in his mind and he had instinctively known.

He snorted.

He couldn't even remember what Palmer looked like, it was so long ago. He might have changed a great deal since then.

Martin Holmberg was no longer frightened, nor did he even feel hatred. He was only infernally tired of it all and wanted to put an end to it.

He leaned right back in his chair and looked up at the ceiling.

HOLY NIGHT

GUNNAR PALMER.

It had begun back in 1969.

But it clearly isn't over yet, thought Martin Holmberg.

At 0057 hours on Christmas Eve of that year, a man had been found dead on the corner between Sand Street and Paradise Street. The dead man had no identification. All he had had on him was a small pocket diary. With the help of the notes in it the police had managed to establish his identity, but not until Tuesday the thirtieth of January.

By chance, that was the same day Holmberg had managed to find the driver of the car. He had splinters of glass from the headlights to work on, and one headlight that had come off. Patiently he had phoned all the garages in Malmo, Eslov, Hoor, Horby, Trelleborg and Lund to ask whether any car with such damage had been left for repair. All the replies had been negative. But then suddenly a firm in Malmo had informed him that they had had a car in for repair. With just that damage.

That was how Martin Holmberg had first come into contact with Gunnar Palmer.

All the indications were that it had been an accident. The man who had been run down and killed—Bo Westin—had simply been unlucky in that he had slipped on the icy street right in the path of Palmer's car.

But then a dead girl had been found in a trunk in a shelter in one of the student residences in the area.

Boel Andersson had been strangled on the night between the third and fourth of January. She had known Bo Westin. She had known Gunnar Palmer and she had been sitting beside Palmer in the car that had hit Westin.

Boel Andersson had been a student, but in addition had worked at a porn club in Malmo, and she had also helped Palmer sexually in return for money.

Boel Andersson's remarkable nymphomaniac sex life had been revealed during the investigation. It was a strange mixture of self-degradation and inordinate enjoyment that had expressed itself in her playing games with her various partners, using her body as a bait.

Gunnar Palmer had been caught on her hook. His emotional and sexual life was at least as complicated as Boel's.

He was a history graduate and was writing a thesis on the Second World War in Swedish Literature. He lived alone in an apartment on Erik Dahlberg Street. He was an introverted and complicated person, timid and isolated. His wife had died in childbirth in '65, and so had the child. That was what had tied him in emotional knots.

He had never recovered from the trauma.

His sexual life since the death of his wife had been with prostitutes. Boel Andersson had been one of them, a hundred kronor a time, at least once a week, sometimes twice. In addition, he had fallen in love with her. But she had not fallen in love with him. To her, he was nothing but one customer among many.

Her interest was in money, a lot of money, quick money.

So she worked as a stripper in a club in Malmo, took parts in pornographic films and sold her body.

All the indications were that Gunnar Palmer had strangled Boel Andersson out of a kind of jealousy that might have been desperation because he could no longer endure her playing with his feelings, mauling them and making money out of it.

After the lengthy interrogations Palmer had been not only crushed but actually broken when he was forced to make public his sexual isolation and difficulties in finding partners, as well as his nightmarish loneliness.

But Palmer had not been guilty of the girl's murder.

A frightened unsuspecting Palmer had been taken to the police station for questioning on that day in January, 1970. A bowed and broken Palmer had finally left it.

It should have been all over then.

But it wasn't.

He could expect a charge of causing death and failing to stop after an accident. So he was arrested and again taken to the police station. He was kept in custody on remand for three days and then had had to wait six weeks for his case to come up. He was not taken into custody again. The court sentenced him to three months. His sentence was appealed and changed to a suspended sentence. The prosecutor asked for this to be reversed, but that was refused. In addition to the suspended sentence, he was fined five hundred kronor and banned from driving for two years.

That was all Martin Holmberg knew about Gunnar Palmer. He had no idea what had happened to him since, nor did he even know whether he had moved away from Lund. For him, Gunnar Palmer had been a completed case as soon as he had been brought to court.

He had never given him a thought during the intervening years.

When the Palmer case had been on, he had felt sympathy for him, regarding him as an unhappy person whom life had ill-treated and who never seemed to be able to escape misfortune. He had felt compassion for him because he seemed to him a tragic figure, a small tragic harmless nobody, whom life and circumstances had treated badly.

He could smell burning.

He switched on the desk lamp. His cigarette had burned down to the filter and the ash was lying on the floor. He flung the filter into the ashtray and rubbed his face with the palms of his hands. Then he picked up the telephone receiver and started dialing his home number, but stopped on the last number and pressed down the button.

What was Olofsson's home number again?

He had to look it up.

Boel answered.

"Hi, it's Martin. How are things?"

"Fine, but how are things with *you*, poor dears?"

"Things are happening. At least we know who it is now. Gunnar Palmer. Does that mean anything to you?"

"No. Do you want to talk to Kerstin?"

"Yes, please."

"She's just coming. The children have had a fine time. Your kids are really great. Pity you...oh, here's Kerstin. See you on Boxing Day."

"Before that, I hope. But thanks a lot. See you later."

"Martin?"

"Hi," he said. "How's everything?"

"Under the circumstances...."

"Hmm. Well, at least I know you're safe and okay where you are."

He looked at the photograph of the children on his desk.

"It's Gunnar Palmer who's plaguing the life out of us," he

said. "His latest effort was to throw a stone through our kitchen window."

"What?"

Martin told her.

Kerstin was silent for a long time. "Poor devil," she said. "It's quite hard to hate him for what he's done."

"Yes. But we must put a stop to it. We'll have to track him down and lure him out. Wherever he may be."

"Can we go home tomorrow? The kids keep asking about their presents. I forgot to take them with me in the muddle of leaving."

"I think so. Yes, I'm sure you can. Now we know who it is, it's not so threatening any longer. Tell them they can have their presents tomorrow. Are they asleep?"

"No, of course not. It's Christmas Eve."

They talked for ten minutes. Then he phoned the police station in Himmelsholm and was given Elg's home number.

Elg's voice sounded slurred when he answered.

ROSEN WENT BACK to the police station alone in time to sign off. He explained why Fransson was not with him.

The child was asleep in bed, but every time Fransson reached the door to slip out, she instinctively woke up. She sat up and seeing him over by the door and realizing he was leaving, started screaming the place down, refusing to calm down until he went back to her bed and sat down on the chair again. She did not go to sleep again until she had several times made quite sure he was really sitting there.

Fransson had given up in the end.

"I'll have to stay, I suppose."

"Let the kid scream," Rosen had said. "She'll soon quiet down and go to sleep."

"No, I haven't the heart or stomach to do that. Would you call my wife and tell her what's happened?"

Rosen had no irresistible desire to pass the message on, so he asked one of the other men to do it. He must have explained the situation badly, or the other man had misunderstood the whole affair, because Mrs. Fransson was appalled to hear that her husband was in the Children's Clinic. She at once got into the car with their son and went to visit Fransson there in his sickbed.

She was in a very aggressive mood when she finally left the clinic. But once she was back home she couldn't go on being angry and saw the comical side of the situation.

She phoned the clinic and was put through to a nurse who couldn't make out what she meant when she said, "This is Mrs. Fransson. Would you mind telling my husband I'm not angry with him?"

The nurse had no idea what she was talking about.

They had no Fransson working at the clinic, and no patient called Fransson in her department old enough to be married. The eldest patient was fourteen and he had severe internal pains.

John Fransson was sitting by the child's bed trying to work out how he could make his wife happy again.

He understood that his own son was disappointed he wasn't at home on Christmas Eve as a father should be. But she ought to have learned by now that unexpected situations arose. He had been a policeman for eleven years and married to her for twelve. She ought to know better.

He sat there getting more and more annoyed with her, the more he thought about it.

BEFORE OLOFSSON, MANSSON AND WESTERBERG left Myrtle Walde's apartment, they searched her drawers and read through the letters she had kept. They had gone through everything that might give them a clue.

But they found nothing of any value.

The few letters Myrtle had kept were from her mother, who lived in Umea in the far north, or from a photographer in a fashion firm, or from women friends. There were a great many postcards. She seemed to have kept all the postcards she received, both from abroad and from various places around the country. There were two large boxes full of them, five albums full of postcards, and nine albums not yet filled.

They found the baptismal certificate in a drawer. The little girl was called Anna-Maria. She was eighteen months and nine days old.

Salary slips from the post office were in a loose-leaf file, as well as records of payments from the fashion firm, and also a statement from a magazine that three thousand kronor had been paid for photographic reproduction rights.

But they found no threatening letters, nor anything that helped them in any way. They placed their hopes in the address book.

They tore out the pages. Olofsson took A to H, Mansson I to P, and Westerberg Q to Z.

Olofsson made nineteen calls, Mansson thirty-one and Westerberg twelve.

They learned nothing of great value. Most people replied and were appalled to hear that something had happened to Myrtle. But they did find out a little.

Myrtle was a girl who worked hard to support her daughter. She was even considered rather miserly, or at best careful with her money. She liked an evening out now and again and occasionally enjoyed herself modestly with a girl friend from the post office. They went dancing, sharing a bottle of wine and eating simply. Sometimes they went to a smarter place, but Myrtle never accepted suggestions and never went back with men. She had to get back to relieve the baby-sitter.

Myrtle had no steady boyfriend. She was thirty years old, had come to Lund seven years before and had worked at the post office on the counter ever since. No one knew who the father of her child was. But she had gone out for a while with someone who had gone off to be a soldier with the United Nations Forces. That had been about two years ago, slightly more, sometime in the autumn of '75. No one could remember what his name was.

Myrtle, to the delight of all her male colleagues at work, had once been the centre pinup of the summer issue of a popular magazine. Her women colleagues had either screwed up their noses or not thought it particularly remarkable. She had been called Vera in the magazine and was said to be working in an office in Skovde. But the mailman, who used to take a break to study the latest numbers of all the magazines in the mail, had recognized her and announced the fact far and wide.

Myrtle could not be said to be flirtatious. No one knew anything about her sex life, at least that was what the people they spoke to said. Although in some way she must have arranged for that part of her life, clearly she did so discreetly. She was by no means considered to be man-mad.

General opinion was that she was an intelligent girl who knew her way around, knew how to take care of herself, managed on her own, answered back if necessary, had principles, as one mailman with staff-party experience had informed them, and was generally liked all around.

There was simply nothing whatsoever remarkable about Myrtle Walde's life that would explain why she had left her apartment, abandoned her child and disappeared.

"Could it be someone who's seen those nude pictures and is a mad pervert and won't stop until—"

"No," said Olofsson.

They were tired out after all that telephoning and depressed by the minimal results.

"The point is, are we getting anywhere?" sighed Westerberg. "A perfectly ordinary girl... what can have happened?"

He shook his head.

He pulled faces, trying to reach a few mustache hairs to chew, but as it was a new growth he did not meet with much success.

Olofsson rose with a groan, stretching and yawning so that his eyes watered.

"I wonder what Martin's up to?" he said.

He went to find out.

Holmberg's office was in darkness, but the air was thick with cigarette smoke and the ashtray overflowing with butts. The telephone directory was lying open on his desk.

Olofsson switched the light on and looked at it. It lay open at the yellow pages, hotels and boarding hourses.

He scratched the back of his neck.

What had Martin found out?

He dialed a number on the intercom.

"Yes?" said the duty officer.

"Anyone down there know where Martin's got to?"

"No, I haven't seen him. Wait—"

Olofsson heard him calling, "Anyone know where Martin Holmberg is?"

"No, no one here knows."

"Thanks."

He went back to Mansson and Westerberg.

"He's disappeared," he said.

"Has he got hold of something?" said Mansson.

"Don't ask me," said Olofsson.

"What do we do now?" said Westerberg.

"Get some sleep. We need it."

"I'm going back home to sleep," said Mansson. "I've a spare sofa if that interests anyone."

"The sofa here will do for me," said Olofsson, sitting down and starting to undo his laces.

"Okay," said Westerberg. "I've slept on your sofa before. When do we meet again?"

Olofsson looked at his watch.

Quarter past three.

"Eight o'clock, here," he said. "If anything happens I'll phone and wake you."

Mansson lived on Cloister Street, not far from the police station. Mansson and Westerberg left.

Olofsson lay down, closed his eyes and fell asleep.

He snored loudly.

Outside, the night was absolutely silent and still, with no wind at all; a cold clear night of high pure air, the full moon making the white snow glitter.

Olofsson was still sleeping when people started waking up to go to early service or switch on their television sets to enjoy the early service broadcast on Christmas morning.

Fransson was asleep on his chair at the clinic.

But not everyone was alseep.

Doctors and nurses at the hospital were busy with gall-stones and people's pains and injuries. The police dealt with five drunks, three domestic disturbances, and two burglars were caught red-handed, a third after information was received.

On the whole it had been a quiet night.

In Lund.

23

ALL YOUR WISHES
WILL BE GRANTED

MARTIN BEGAN with the most logical thing to do, telephoning all the hotels in Lund. First he described Palmer from the seven-year-old photograph he had found in the archives. There was no guest corresponding to that in any hotel in town.

Where should he go on to now? Malmo?

He had been successful there the last time. Why not this time, too?

So . . . Malmo.

He began with the *ABC Travel and Hotel Guide* and lost count at about the fortieth call. But when he had dialed about the fiftieth number, repeating the same question in a tired hoarse voice, he was given a positive answer. Palmer was living under his own name at the Silver Hotel in Malo.

He had never heard of it.

His first reaction was to leap out of his chair, rush for the door, run down to the car and set off with tires screaming.

He slowly put the receiver down and propped his elbows on his desk, clasping his hands and resting his chin on them as he stared at the opposite wall.

An expectant tension began to make itself felt within him, combined with some hesitation and uncertainty.

Naturally, he ought to tell Seved.

Naturally, he should alert the force in Malmo and get them to go and pick up Palmer.

But somehow this was a private matter—a war between him and the other man, a war in which the other man was the aggressor and he the innocent victim.

There was that, of course: just how innocent was he? No one was attacked without reason. There was always something motivating the attacker.

He could not judge how guilty he was personally, and he

didn't think Palmer's attacks were directed against him personally. He presumed what Palmer was attacking was a symbol of the system, the machinery of justice that had castrated him as a human being and an individual. And the most concrete face in the confusion of titles and officials, from policemen to judge, happened to be his.

He wanted to meet Palmer in peace and quiet, to talk to him, to talk sense to him.

And explain.

Explaining that he had only been doing his duty on that occasion seven years ago. Explaining that he had been genuinely sorry if it had led to breaking Palmer as a person, owing to the suffering a long-drawn-out trial had entailed.

He wanted to talk to him and he wanted them to part as two human beings who understood each other, and that would be the end of it.

Elg had told him about the cat Palmer had drowned.

The thought that Palmer and Jack the Dog Ripper were the same person had struck him, but he had brushed it aside. It did not fit the picture of the man he remembered. Though, of course, a person can change over so many years, depending on the circumstances.

He couldn't for the life of him understand why Palmer should direct his revenge onto him on two fronts, so to speak; partly directly in the form of cards, telephone calls and stone throwing, and partly by killing animals, which could hardly be described as attacking him.

He rose and started putting on his jacket, but then stopped and put it down on his desk. He took off his holster and put it into a desk drawer, closed the drawer and locked it. Then he put on his jacket and overcoat and thrust his gun into his coat pocket. He turned the light out and closed the door behind him.

He walked slowly past Olofsson's door and stopped to listen. Seved seemed to be talking.

No, he decided. This was a matter between him and Palmer.

The man who had come rushing out of the apartment house in North Vall Street had not been Palmer, according to Sture Kvist.

Holmberg's car was over in the parking lot alongside the access down into the police station underground lot. He drove straight through the empty town to the Dalby traffic circle, then swung down onto the highway.

He was driving toward Malmo.

HE PARKED THE CAR outside the pharmacy in Great Square, went through the passage that came out onto Calendar Street, and just as he emerged he saw the hotel sign. He pressed the night bell and several minutes went by before a sleepy and bemused night porter opened the door.

"We're full up," he said. "No rooms. . . ."

"I don't want a room. I want to see someone living here."

"People here don't have visitors at this time of night."

He started closing the door, but Holmberg swiftly put out his foot and held it up against the door.

"The person I want will see me," he said.

"Go away now," said the night porter. "Otherwise I'll call the police. Don't go trying anything. I've got a dog here."

Holmberg sensed he was lying.

He fumbled in his trouser pocket, where he usually kept his change, and his fingers touched paper. He pulled it out. A fifty-kronor note.

"Here," he said. "Take this, and thanks for your trouble."

The night porter looked from him to the note and then back again.

"Who do you want to see?" he said.

"Someone who lives here."

"How do you know she lives here?"

"Who said it was a woman?"

"A man?"

The night porter filled the doorway, so Holmberg could not get in without moving him by force.

"Couldn't you take this now, and move over so I can get by?" he said.

"How do I know you're not going to cause a disturbance?"

"I'm from the police," said Holmberg, taking out his identity card.

The night porter started.

"Why didn't you say so, then? Why all this secrecy? Are you a secret agent or something?"

"No," said Holmberg, smiling. "But it's a rather sensitive matter."

"I see," said the night porter, nodding with incomprehension.

He looked greedily at the note Holmberg was putting back in his pocket, then sighed and moved to one side.

"Do you know which room he's in?"

"Yes," said Holmberg. He started up the stairs.

"He's in number seven," the night porter had said earlier over the telephone.

He came to the door. Should he knock, and wait for Palmer to open up?

Holmberg looked at his watch: twenty to three. Presumably Palmer was asleep.

He went on past two more doors and came to the end of the corridor, where there was a glass door, a balcony outside it. He opened the door and stepped out. It was a wide balcony with a gap between the railings on the right and the gable of the building.

He turned around and looked at the balcony door handle. It could be opened from the outside.

He leaned over the railing and by holding onto the drainpipe he could see around the gable. A balcony ran all along past the rooms, divided up accordingly. A wide ledge ran around the gable.

He got up onto the railing, grasped the drainpipe, the metal icy cold on his bare hands. He leaned forward and pressed the top half of his body against the drainpipe. He felt with his left foot down to the ledge, then was forced to let the other foot go the same way. The next moment he was standing on the ledge. He was aware of his feet slipping and with a firm grip on the drainpipe he made his way around the gable and found a foothold on the ledge on the other side.

He kept as close to the balcony as he could, still holding onto the drainpipe, stretching out his left hand to get a hold on the railing. He pulled himself close to the railing, heaved himself quickly up and found himself standing on the balcony.

He was breathing heavily and could feel the cold biting through his clothes. His body was trembling and his arms and legs shaking. He was sweating profusely, making the cold seem even worse.

Now let me see. I walked past two doors.

He climbed up on the railing and without difficulty got down on the other side.

The next one.

He looked at the window. It was dark and the blind was up, so presumably the room was not in use.

Then he repeated the maneuver and found himself on the balcony of room seven. The blind was down, not a glimmer of light around the edges of it. He felt the balcony-door handle. It wouldn't budge.

Safety catch.

He shook his head and stood alongside the balcony's glass door. Then he measured with his elbow and struck. There was a crash as the glass splintered and his elbow hurt.

He thrust his hand inside and fumbled for the catch on the inside. There was no bolt. He found the catch and turned it, trying to open the balcony door at the same time. But it wouldn't move. He released the pressure on the handle and now he could turn the safety catch and then open the door.

He opened it slowly and cautiously.

He's already heard me, he thought, pulling side the blind as he jerked open the door and stepped into the room.

He was aware of a movement diagonally behind him, but had no time to react.

PALMER LOOKED AT THE MAN who had collapsed when the wooden chair had landed on top of his head. He looked at the chair, which had remained whole, and put it down. He went over to the door and switched on the overhead light. The fallen man was lying on his side.

He was frightened and did not know what to do.

Then he realized there was something familiar about the figure lying there. He went over and carefully turned him over onto his back. He let out a short laugh . . . but then felt panic, wanting to turn and run. Something was sticking out of Holmberg's coat pocket, something that had almost fallen out. He picked it up and held the weapon in his hand.

He was sitting on the bed with his legs drawn up underneath him and the gun pointing at the policeman when the latter slowly opened his eyes and put his hand up to his head.

Martin turned his head. It hurt at the back and there was an unnatural thumping in his temples. Through a mist he saw the figure sitting on the bed, and he hauled himself to his knees.

He shook his head, but that only increased the pain.

He kept his head still and breathed deeply.

He tried to get up, but his legs refused to function. Finally he managed to get to his knees.

Gradually and very slowly his vision cleared, but contours were blurred and some time went by before he was aware of the gun pointing at him.

He stretched out his hand.

"Give it here," he said briefly and hoarsely.

Palmer just went on looking at him.

Holmberg made another attempt to get up, but his legs gave away under him again and he fell heavily to the floor.

Palmer looked at him as he lay there unmoving on his back, breathing heavily as if he were sleeping. The corners of his mouth were jerking and a trickle of blood was coming out of one nostril.

Palmer rose, went over to the body and raised the gun, aiming it at the head, his finger resting rigidly on the trigger.

This is what I've been waiting for. Now revenge is mine.

He could feel a trembling agitation that made his fingertips tingle and his scalp prickle.

He tried to press the trigger, but nothing happened. He looked at the gun in surprise, then threw it aside with an oath that was half a sob.

He went over to the table and took the top off the bottle, filled the tooth glass and gulped down the whiskey.

Then he sank down on the chair as the alcohol took effect, making him shudder.

He could feel the cold from the balcony door, so he closed it. But it was still cold. His pajamas were thin, so he took them off and put on his underclothes, polo-necked sweater and trousers, pulled on his socks and laced his shoes.

Then he sat down on the edge of the bed, put his hands on his knees and looked at the unconscious Holmberg.

He could not think. He could only register the fact that the man at whom his hatred had been more and more directed was now lying defenseless on the floor.

He just sat there looking.

HE WAS STILL SITTING THERE twenty minutes later when Martin opened his eyes and managed to stagger to his feet.

"How do you feel?" said Palmer.

"Hellish," said Holmberg, going over to the washbasin.

He took a towel, soaked it in cold water and held it against the back of his head.

"You ought to go to hospital. Concussion—"

"Time enough. We've got a lot to talk about first."

He put his hand into his coat pocket and realized the gun had gone.

He looked at Palmer and saw him glance away. The gun was lying at the end of the bed, right by the wall.

Palmer shook his head slowly and stretched his hand out toward it. He put the gun in his lap.

"Talk about what?" he said.

"About you."

Holmberg sat down on the chair, nudging the bottle as he put his elbow on the table, then pulling both bottle and glass toward him. He poured out some whiskey and gulped it down, but it did not affect his headache.

Palmer was not the Palmer he remembered.

He remembered a bowed figure shuffling into the garage, a man well wrapped up against the cold. He remembered a diffident, almost servile man, bitterly relating the qualms he had been through after having killed a person with his car. He remembered a smooth-shaven, pedantic, prudent person, who had become more and more bowed, sinking farther and farther down into the chair during long and exhausting interrogations. He remembered a small frightened person, who nevertheless had seemed pleased to be able to unburden his conscience, but appeared pitifully broken when he was forced to admit what had happened to his sexual life after his wife's death.

The man he now saw was slightly more crumpled and fatter than seven years ago, his face lined and cheeks sunken, his beard bushy and wild, his hair unbrushed and untidy. And his eyes.

He did not recognize the eyes, either.

The man he remembered had had living eyes, eyes that had pleaded, eyes that had explained that his soul was seared, eyes that had become sorrowful or aggressive. Eyes that had flickered, red eyes with black rings under them.

The eyes were dead now, the look in them stony. Hard, frozen eyes. Indifferent eyes, but wide open all the same, searching.

There was a slyness in them now, a cunning in his judging eyes.

"What do you really want?" said Holmberg.

Palmer did not reply, but only swayed back and forth slightly.

"Why did you drown your cat?"

"Should I have left it to starve to death?"

"You're sick, Gunnar. Do you know that?"

The eyes froze, staring, apparently looking straight through him.

"What I find difficult to understand is why a person like

you, who's had a bad time, wants to cause someone else suffering?''

Palmer laughed. ''Difficult to understand!'' he repeated ironically. ''I'd have thought it was quite easy.''

''What happened after your sentence?''

''What sentence?''

''Causing death. You killed him...I can't remember his name.''

''Westin. Bo Westin.''

''That's it. You were given a suspended sentence and fined. Nothing dreadful about that.''

''Maybe not, no.''

''Why didn't you go on with your thesis?''

Palmer's eyes looked straight through him again.

''What thesis?''

''You didn't have to go to prison. You could've gone on with it.''

''Could I? Maybe, yes.''

''It was your nightly walks that made me find you.''

''What nightly walks?''

''You moved to Himmelsholm and became a school care-taker.''

''Yes, one has to do something.''

''When did you move?''

''In '72.''

''You're a man of habit. Night after night you went for the same walk, then stood on the same street corner. Then you turned around and went to a square in that town and bought a hot dog. Then you went home, but another way.''

''So what?''

''They missed you when you stopped.''

''They?''

''The people who wondered why you came and stood on that corner. I've never been to Himmelsholm. What was special about that corner?''

''It was almost the same.''

''As the corner of Paradise Street and Sand Street?''

Palmer nodded, with the look of a defiant schoolboy forced to admit to his friends that he had masturbated in the lavatory in the dinner hour.

''Some people found out where you lived. And then I heard the police were looking for you.''

Palmer laughed his hollow laugh.

"The police," he said. "I suppose you know what time of day I crap, too?"

"It was the cat. Someone wondered what had happened to your cat when you went away. And the police went in to look."

"Oh, yes."

"When I met you seven years ago, you had cleared away every single thing that might remind you of your wife, who had died five years before. According to the Himmelsholm police there was nothing, absolutely nothing personal in your apartment."

"No, I've cleared the last few years out of my life. Those years are dead."

"What were you going to do next?"

Palmer did not reply.

"Telephone terrorism, letter terrorism, stone throwing. What were you going to do next? When were you going to stop?"

"Stop?"

"Were you going to set fire to my house!" Martin almost shouted.

"Yes," said Palmer calmly.

Holmberg shuddered, poured out another finger of whiskey and took a gulp.

"What did you hope to achieve?" he said. "Did you want to kill me and my family?"

"I wanted you to suffer. For what so-called justice had done to me."

"But Gunnar, you killed a man. That was why you were punished."

"Yes."

"You're sick, Gunnar. How long were you going to let me suffer, then?"

"Until you couldn't stand it any longer. . . ."

"What are you going to do now?"

"What do you mean, do?"

"You're surely not going to go on phoning my home and saying nothing when someone answers? Surely you're not going to go on sending letters? Surely you're not going to go on throwing stones?"

"Why not?"

"Do you really mean you were going to set fire to my house?"

"Yes."

"But it's in a terrace. The whole lot could have burned down."

"So what?"

"Don't you mind if people are hurt or die?"

"Why should I?"

"I came here because I thought we'd be able to talk this out and understand one another."

"Oh, yes."

"That time when you ran down Westin, I was forced to find you to discover what had happened. I was only doing my job."

"That's your affair."

"But *you* ran him down!"

"That's my affair."

"Is it that business with Boel? Can't you get over her dying?"

"Yes, I've got over that."

"But you can't forgive that you were suspected?"

He did not reply.

"I don't understand you," said Holmberg. "How long were you going to keep terrorizing me?"

"Always."

"You're sick, Gunnar. You're dangerous, too. Dangerous to yourself more than anyone else. You're destroying yourself."

"I'm not the one destroying myself."

"Now you're bitter because you were forced to accept the punishment for what you did?"

"No, for what you did to me."

"Gunnar, I want us to part here, and I want you to promise to stop terrorizing me and my family. Go back to your own life. Take up your thesis again. Try to start living again."

"Living. . . ." It sounded like a dead word in his mouth.

"Why did you move away from Lund?"

"Because I didn't want to stay."

"Why not?"

"Because I couldn't stand it. There was no point."

"I can take you with me now. To the police station. Do you know what that involves? It involves you going to court again and being charged with making illegal threats. You'd probably get a mild sentence after a psychiatric report. Presumably some psychiatric treatment. You'll almost certainly be confined to hospital for a while. And then when you come out again, what'll it be like then? Have you thought about that?"

"No."

"What have you thought about at all?"

"You."

"You hate the police and the courts, which you think have been unjust to you, and you want retribution to fall on me?"

"You were the cause of it."

"Because I found you?"

"You found me and then . . . it started. What do you think it's like having your dirty linen washed in public?" he shouted suddenly. "What do you think it's like sitting on a chair surrounded by a crowd of snotty policemen enjoying forcing me to tell them about my . . . my loneliness. What do you think it's like being suspected of killing the only person I've ever loved . . . since *she* died?"

"Your wife?"

"Yes."

"Why just Himmelsholm?"

"I wanted to get away from Lund."

"And in all those years in Himmelsholm, your hatred grew and grew, and you couldn't stop thinking about what had happened, so you returned to Lund to get your own back?"

"You should know what it means to suffer."

"Do you think I'm going to let you terrorize my family?"

"No, of course not."

Palmer picked up the gun.

"If you'd had this, you'd have shot me to make sure of stopping me, wouldn't you?" he said.

"No."

"Huh! You're so big and strong. You're so powerful, with your guns and your authority. You've got power! Power over people! Power to force us into degradation. Power to crush us and humble us. But you never think of what the consequences might be."

"For whom?"

"You'll see," said Palmer.

"No, I won't. Because there's going to be an end to your terrorizing here and now."

Palmer raised the gun and aimed it straight at Holmberg.

"And what if I shoot you? Then your wife and children will suffer even more without big strong daddy policeman to protect them."

"You can't. The safety catch is on."

Palmer looked away.

"I know," he said quietly. "I've thought up a great many refined ways of letting you and your family really know what suffering means. What you've seen is only a start."

"How is your mother?"

Palmer started.

"She's dead," he said.

"I'm sorry to hear that."

"She died three years ago. But she didn't know anything about what happened to me. Though I don't suppose she would have understood. Her mind had quite gone over the last few years."

"Are you very lonely?"

"Yes."

"No friends?"

"Alone. And strong."

"That's the most dangerous idea of all, that one is alone and strong."

"It's a fact."

"What do the girls cost in Himmelsholm?" said Holmberg, trying another tack. "I'm sure they don't let you sleep with them for free, those country tarts."

Palmer began to shake.

"You feeble little shit," said Holmberg. "You think you can crush me and my family and have peace in your withered little soul!"

"Shut up!"

"Don't you ever think about Bo Westin? Hadn't he a right to live?"

"It wasn't my fault. He fell in front of the car."

"You weren't paying attention."

"Boel put her hand on my thigh and I accelerated involuntarily. There was no time to brake."

"Did you hate Boel for that? And because she took money for it?"

Palmer didn't reply.

He fingered the gun and Holmberg got up.

"Give it to me now," he said.

"Sit still!" said Palmer.

"Hand it over!" he said.

"Don't!"

There was a loud crack. He had happened to release the safety catch.

Holmberg felt his hand burning.

Everything turned black before his eyes, but he forced himself to look.

Palmer was backing slowly toward the door, the gun pointing at him.

Holmberg's hand felt numb and sticky. The bullet had gone right through it.

"What are you going to do?" he said.

"Your suffering isn't over," said Palmer.

Holmberg looked into his eyes and what he saw frightened him.

He could see a bottomless hatred, but also something he had seen before, a fanatical glow.

"You're crazy," he said.

He lowered his eyes and saw Palmer's fingers whiten. He threw himself down and the bullet went through the window. He heard the key being turned in the lock, and he started getting up. Palmer shot again, hitting the wall this time, a few feet above Martin's head.

He heard Palmer opening the door. Martin raised his head but hurriedly ducked again as the bullet smashed into the bedside lamp.

Then the door slammed and he heard running footsteps.

He got to his knees and looked at his hand. He picked up the wet towel and wound it around his hand, which felt numb, stiff and dead.

He heard a shot from down in the foyer.

He rushed over to the door and out, then down the stairs. The night porter was sitting on the floor, looking at him.

"Are you hurt?" said Holmberg.

"No...but he shot at me...."

Holmberg ran out through the door.

He could hear Palmer's footsteps echoing along the passageway and ran after them. When he got to the square he saw Palmer running across the square toward a car.

He unlocked his own car and jumped in.

The towel had got tangled and he fumbled for a long time before he could get the key out of his pocket. Then he switched on and the engine leaped into life.

Palmer swung down past Kramer, heading in the Lund direction.

Holmberg stepped on the accelerator.

His hand had begun to hurt now, making driving difficult.

The roads were slippery. He ought to alert his colleagues

and get help. But it was still a private matter between him and Palmer.

He was quite far behind when he got onto the highway.

They were the only two cars on the road.

He was driving fast, but could not gain on Palmer.

The hell of it was that he could understand him.

The loner destroyed and bitter, burying himself in his thoughts...seeing in revenge the only chance of self-realization since everything had been taken away from him. The loner living for nothing else except to keep his hatred burning.

His neighbors had, of course, known what had happened when he returned after being questioned. The police had been forced to make inquiries about him from them. They had looked askance at him. Of course they had talked about him behind his back, no doubt so that he heard. Then they had finally stopped speaking to him, forcing him to move, simply by their attitude toward him. Or had he been given notice? And his friends at the institute...if he had had any. The people who had worked there. They had known, of course. And looked. And talked. And avoided him. And then all his memories, the memories of Lund, which had followed him to Himmelsholm....

No, he thought. I mustn't start being sentimental.

By sheer chance Holmberg happened to see Palmer turning off the circle and heading in toward the center of Lund.

He must stop him. Even if he had to kill him. Even if he had to die himself.

There was a burning pain in his hand now. He wondered how much blood he had lost and how clearly he would be able to think.

The clock on the tower of the cathedral struck half-past five.

24

STAR IN THE UNIVERSE

AT 2255 HOURS on Christmas Eve a young woman collapsed just by the Sege traffic circle on the outskirts of Malmo. Ten minutes later she was seen lying on the verge by a passing motorist, who phoned the police from a kiosk in Gustaf Adolf Square and told them. He refused to give his name, maintaining it was nothing to do with him. He described where she was lying.

At 2335 hours the police found the woman and established that she was still alive. They summoned an ambulance that took the deeply unconscious woman to Malmo General Hospital, usually known as M.G.H.

The woman was taken to the casualty department where they found that her unconscious state was due to exhaustion. Her feet were badly frost damaged. One cheek also showed signs of frostbite, but otherwise she seemed to be in a good state of health.

She was taken up to a ward, put on a drip and her frostbite treated. Her possessions were put away and a watcher stationed by her bed.

As she was unconscious and the doctor said it would be several hours before she would come round, the police left the hospital, saying they would come back. It was possible that the woman had been the victim of a crime and her assailant would have to be found, but as they would have to speak to her first to ask her why she had been lying in the snow, all they could do was wait.

If the woman had had any identification documents on her, they could have gone to her home address to make sure all was well there. But there was nothing in the woman's purse to tell them who she was or where she lived.

At a quarter past three the watcher beside the bed woke with a start to hear the woman speaking deliriously. The watcher was a light sleeper.

"He . . . he mustn't . . . mustn't . . ." the woman was mumbling.

The watcher called the nurse and the nurse called the doctor, who hurried into the ward.

The woman had opened her eyes.

"Where am I?" she said.

"You're perfectly safe," said the doctor. "I'm going to give you something to make you sleep now, then we can talk tomorrow."

"But . . . but where am I?" she said, looking from the doctor to the nurse, then to the watcher and around the ward.

"You're in hospital."

"Yes, I can see that. But where?"

"In Malmo, of course."

"In Malmo!"

She grasped the doctor's arm.

"You must help me," she pleaded. "How did I get here?"

"The police—"

"The police?" she said. "They've found her, I suppose?"

"Found who? Has someone disappeared?"

"No . . . but I left her in the car for them to find her."

"Who?"

"Anna-Maria," she said shrilly.

"Who's that?"

"My daughter, of course."

"Why did you leave her there?"

"Because he . . . they've found her, have they?"

"Do you want to speak to the police?"

"Yes, please. Are they here?"

"I'll tell them."

The doctor patted her hand and smiled encouragingly.

"It'll be all right, you'll see."

He went into his office and phoned the police.

Mansson of the Crime Squad was on duty and promised to come.

"What's her name, by the way?" he said.

"I don't know. I forgot to ask."

Mansson asked when he got there.

"Myrtle Walde," she said.

"Where do you live?"

"In Lund."

"In Lund? Then what in heaven's name were you doing in the snowdrifts outside Malmo?"

But as he asked the question, he remembered the message

that had come through from Lund. And when she had briefly explained, he hurried to phone the Lund police station.

Fourteen minutes later Olofsson was woken by the telephone.

"Hi!" said Mansson into his ear. "They told me you were
there. This is Mansson in Malmo, Crime Squad."

"Yes."

"That Walde you were looking for. We've got her here."

Olofsson was given a swift explanation, after which he
hurriedly phoned home to Mansson—his Mansson, as he
occasionally called him to differentiate him from his friend
in Malmo. At thirteen minutes to five Olofsson, Mansson
and Westerberg were at the hospital.

The four policemen sat on chairs around her bed.

She was pale, her hair straggly against the pillow and her
voice thin. But she was quite lucid, although the fear and
anxiety in her voice occasionally came through.

"I was terrified of him doing Anna-Maria some harm,"
she said. "Are you certain you've got her quite safe?"

"Yes," said Olofsson. "She's sound asleep at the Children's Clinic. She's in no danger at all. But how could you
leave her like that?"

"But I phoned you and told you where she was."

"Who is it you're so frightened of?"

"It's rather a long story, really. I haven't dared poke my
nose outside the door since he appeared."

"Take it easy now, and start from the beginning."

She had met him in the summer of '75, when she had been
on holiday in Greece and he had had two weeks' leave and
had taken the opportunity of going over to the mainland. He
was a United Nations soldier in Cyprus. They had met by
chance and they happened to find they had something in
common. She had knocked over her glass in a bar in Athens,
all over his trousers. When she had apologized and started
mopping up with a table napkin, he had said, "You sound as
if you come from Norrland."

"I do," she had said. "From Umea."

"It's a small world. So do I."

They had both laughed.

"May I offer you a drink to replace the one you spilled?"
he said.

"Oh, you don't have to do that."

"What are you drinking?"

"Rum and coke."

He had been drinking whiskey.

"My name's Hans Clemens, by the way. Well, Hans-Rudolf, actually, but Rudolf's such a ghastly name, I leave it out."

"Clemens?" she said. "From Umea?"

"Yes."

"Did you by any chance know Patrik Walde?"

"The old colonel of the regiment?"

"Yes," she said. "He was my father."

"Do you know who my father was?" he said.

"Yes, he was a captain in father's regiment."

"Well, the world couldn't be much smaller, could it? Don't tell me we met when we were small."

"That wouldn't surprise me," she said. "But I don't remember, anyhow."

"Neither do I. That makes us quits. Are you on holiday?"

"Yes."

She went on now, "So I told him a bit about what I did at home in Lund and he told me about what it was like in Cyprus. He was a United Nations soldier, he said. But he regarded himself as a professional soldier. Or a mercenary, as he sometimes called it."

Noncombatant United Nations forces were constantly on the move, because staying for any length of time in one place brought about a monotony that created a demand for drink to drown the boredom. So a Swedish United Nations soldier was allowed to renew his contract for the same assignment only once. But that regulation was often ignored by the majority of Swedes, who stayed considerably longer than the permitted two periods in the same place. With slight exaggeration it could be said that in her United Nations force Sweden had a mercenary army, at least a professional one.

"He thought it was deadly boring in Cyprus. He told me what it had been like during the war there."

"Did you shoot at people?" she had asked.

"Of course," he laughed. "It wasn't a phony war."

"What does it feel like?"

"Feel like? It was my job. It doesn't feel like anything."

"He told me he lacked excitement," she continued. "It was boring just keeping order."

Hans-Rudolf Clemens had had a taste of action. Of war. Holding his automatic pistol and firing shot after shot at the enemy, he had known the intoxication of power. Then his childhood games became reality, away from the regimental town where his father had very early on initiated him into the mysteries of firearms.

"Well, we met quite often in Athens, but then he went back to Cyprus and I thought that was the last I'd seen of him. Then he appeared in Lund. He had resigned in Cyprus, he told me. He was off to Africa now. He had signed up. So he had come to see me. He was staying at a hotel, as he'd given up his old apartment because it had become too expensive. But he wanted to visit Sweden before setting off on his new assignment. He never told me where he was going—well, he said Africa, but not *where* in Africa. I thought he meant with the United Nations. I didn't find out for a long time that he went to Angola to fight against the communists."

He had stayed for a week in Lund and during that time they had met quite a lot. Then he had gone, leaving an address she could write to.

He had left in July, and a fortnight later she had received a postcard with greetings from Miami Beach. She wrote in August a couple of times, and then she wrote in September telling him that it looked as if she was pregnant. But toward the end of the month she was able to write again and tell him the danger, as she called it, was over. Her period had skipped a month.

That letter had come back in November. It was enclosed in an envelope with a letter saying that Myrtle Walde was the only acquaintance of Hans-Rudolf Clemens the writer had been able to find. The reason her letter had not been delivered to the addressee was that he had been wounded in action against the communist forces from Cuba in Angola.

"So Anna-Maria isn't his child?"

"No."

"Who is the child's father?"

"Does that matter?"

"No, I suppose not."

"Then I won't tell you. But about ten days ago Hans suddenly appeared again. After all this time. It gave me a shock. One evening the doorbell rang and there he was."

"Here's a surprise for you!" he had said.

"Hans! But what on—I mean, aren't you . . .?"

"Dead? No. They can't finish me off as easily as that. Can I come in?"

"Yes, I . . . yes, come on in."

"You don't seem to be exactly dancing for joy to see me back."

"It's so unexpected."

She hadn't wanted him to come in at all, and she tried to fend him off when he went to embrace her, but he was strong and there was an autocratic touch in his manner, a show of strength.

She felt obliged to offer him something.

"Would you like some coffee?"

"Haven't you anything else? Whiskey, maybe?"

"No . . . a little liqueur—"

"Christ, no! Yes—better than nothing."

He had told her about his time in Africa, his eyes glowing as he spoke with relish about being in action and the men he had killed.

There was something frightening in his manner, something that made her wish he would soon go away.

"I killed lots of them," he said. "But then they took me prisoner. I thought they were going to execute me on the spot, but they wanted to squeeze some information out of me. I was a platoon leader, after all."

He told her about the torture he had endured, his powers of resistance, and how he had been locked up and tortured over and over again, until one day the camp had been overwhelmed and the prisoners released. He told her about his long spell in field hospital where they had patched him up, about how deadly boring it had been just lying there unable to do anything. He wanted to get back to the fighting.

To the killing.

He had been a prisoner for five weeks. Then the adventure in Angola had come to an end.

But there were other adventures in Africa. Regiments from other countries wanting to hire mercenaries to fight the guerillas.

And now he had to come home to see the child.

"What child?"

"Mine, of course."

"Yours?"

"Yes, I got your letter. . . ."

"Oh, I see. But you never got my second letter. Nothing came of it. It was a false alarm."

"But—but—the toys? Surely *you* don't play with them?"

"No, my little daughter does."

"The child?"

"Not your child. Mine."

"But it must have a father."

"Yes, but it's not you."

"Who is it, then?"

"I'm not going to tell you."

"I don't believe you."

"You have to. You simply have to believe me. She isn't your child."

"You're lying, and I want to see her. A girl, you say?"

She went on, "I threatened to set the dog on him, but he just laughed and said he would kill it with his bare hands.

"Then my brother appeared, and Hans went away, saying he would be back. My brother suggested I move in with him for the time being. But I didn't want to. He told me I ought to tell the police. But—"

"Why didn't you?" said Westerberg.

"What good would that have done?"

"We could have helped you."

"For how long? You might have arrested him, but he'd have soon been out and he'd have started all over again...."

"It's not that simple," said Olofsson.

But she just shrugged.

"What happened then?"

"Well, I didn't hear from him for several days. I thought he'd gone. But then he started telephoning. He phoned and said he had to see me, and he wanted to see his child. I explained that I wanted to be left alone. I threatened him with the dog and with my brother, but he just laughed and promised he'd show me what he could do to dogs and people."

She could see him sitting in the car outside, down on the street. But he didn't come up and ring the bell.

She dared not go out. She telephoned to work and said she was ill.

She couldn't get help from her brother, as he was abroad and wouldn't be back until Boxing Day.

But Hans kept phoning, constantly repeating his demands.

She threatened him with the dog and her brother.

He laughed and promised her that she would soon know what he was capable of doing to dogs and people.

"Then he phoned one morning and described what he'd done to an Alsatian."

"Bar's dog," said Mansson of Lund, nodding.

"So he's the one who killed those animals we heard about!" exclaimed Mansson of Malmo.

"Obviously," said Olofsson. "So he killed your dog, too."

"Yes. One night he came up and rang the bell. He asked me if I'd read the paper and seen about the Alsatian he'd killed. I was terrified he would break the door down and come in. He told me about the cat he'd hanged, and said that was what would happen to me if I didn't let him see the child. I was petrified and set the dog on him. But—"

"I know what happened to it," said Olofsson. "Why didn't you telephone us?"

She didn't reply.

"It was silly of you not to," he said.

"Yes," she said. "It probably was. But I just wanted to get away from it all."

"Why didn't you go then?" said Mansson of Lund.

"Because I was afraid he would be outside."

Then he had phoned on Christmas Eve and said he was going to kill another dog.

"And when you read about it, remember that whatever happens to the dog will happen to the kid."

"You must be crazy. You're out of your mind!"

"Come on out and see."

A few moments later she had heard a car honking down on the street. She had looked down and seen him getting out. He had looked up at her window and seen the curtain move, then he waved something that looked like a large knife and started walking away.

"That was when I thought that if I was going to run away, that was the moment to do so."

She had packed necessities into a case, dressed the little girl, put her in the carry cot, gone down to her car and set off. The car had stalled outside Central Station. The gas had run out. Someone had emptied the tank and even the reserve tank was empty.

"Why didn't you come to us then?" said Olofsson.

"I wanted to get to Malmo, back to my brother's apartment. I could hide there until he came back and could help me."

"But why didn't you come to us?" persisted Olofsson.

"Would you have killed him?"

"Killed?"

"Yes, that was the only way to get away from him for-

ever. You would have done nothing but arrest him, and
after a while he would have been free again and able to go
on terrorizing me . . . tormenting me. I'm sure he was going
to kill me. And my child."

"What did you do then? When the car stopped?"

"At first I couldn't think what to do. I thought about the
train. But I hadn't enough money with me. I had only a few
coins in my purse because I'd taken the wrong one. I didn't
dare go back home to fetch money. And I couldn't buy a
ticket with the money I had."

So she phoned the police and told them about the child in
the car, so that Anna-Maria would be looked after. Then she
had begun to walk toward Malmo, along the old road.

"I couldn't take Anna-Maria with me when it was so cold.
I'd never have managed it."

She had taken her case, but was forced to abandon that
about half way. She hadn't seen a single car that might have
given her a lift.

When she—and she could no longer think how far she had
walked—finally reached the outskirts of Malmo, her legs
began to give way. She had to get right through Malmo, too,
as her brother lived on the other side of town.

She could no longer feel her feet and she was frozen
through and exhausted. She collapsed. She couldn't even
remember walking the last stretch.

The only thing that had kept her going was the thought of
her brother and that he would kill Hans-Rudolf. Then she
would be at peace.

"What makes you think your brother would do that?"
said Olofsson.

"I knew he'd help me."

"Oh, yes," said Olofsson, doubting whether she believed
what she was saying.

"My brother's a wrestler, one of the best in the country.
He's been in the national team and almost got a medal in the
World Championships. Haven't you heard of him? Kurt
Walde."

"No. But where is he now? You said he was abroad."

"He's a bus driver. He's driving a party to Berlin. People
who're spending Christmas there and coming back on Boxing Day. That's tomorrow, isn't it?"

"Yes. Are you still going to ask your brother to kill
him?"

"I suppose it won't be that easy . . . now that you know."

"No. We'll try to get hold of him. Can you tell us anything that might help us find him?"

"But you won't kill him?"

"No."

"What's the point, then? I mean, he'll be inside for a while, and then he'll be out again and can go on."

"It's not that simple. People judged as dangerous have to be isolated."

"He *is* dangerous. He's sick! He's insane!"

"Tell us now what you know about where we might find him?"

"I don't know. He once said when he phoned that he was living in his car."

"What sort of car has he got?"

"A Volvo sedan. Gray."

It was half-past five when they left her. They had a detailed description of him.

Olofsson promised to talk to the doctor and ask him to see if she might be moved to Lund Hospital so that she could be with Anna-Maria.

"God Almighty, what a story!" sighed Mansson on his way back to Lund. "Now I suppose we've got to find him."

"The question is where?" said Westerberg. "And I'm not armed. We must go via the station."

"Steady now," said Olofsson.

25

IF ONLY THE WORLD
WERE LARGER

HOLMBERG NOTICED he was gaining on Palmer. They had driven straight through the town along Great South Street, then onto Church Street after Great Square, then Broad Street. The tower of the cathedral was floodlit for the early Christmas service.

North Toll. Palmer drove straight through a red light at the crossroads, then onto Geting Road, after which he swung sharply onto King Oscar Road, then over the railway viaduct onto Oresund Road as far as the Fellier circle around it onto Fellier Road, then back into town toward the center again.

Holmberg had kept up. He was about two or three hundred yards behind, traveling at about seventy.

Palmer swung onto Pheasant Road, his tires screaming, then turned onto Trollberg Road at the circle.

A patrol car came nosing out from Builder Street and the driver did not even have time to react until Holmberg had roared past.

"SA Martin Four, SA Martin Four, over!"

"SA Martin Four here. Over."

"SA Martin Four-nine-three. Two cars heading at high speed toward Station Square. We're going after them. Request assistance. Over."

Holmberg glanced into his rearview mirror as he heard the sirens behind him, his hand aching, sweat pouring off him.

How long had they been driving around town? The clock on the dashboard said a quarter to six.

They hurtled straight through Lund, out toward Dalby Road.

At the Dalby circle they swung down onto the highway and headed north, then turned off it at the north access and drove onto Geting Road.

Now they were heading back toward the center again.

Holmberg had two patrol cars behind him now, but to judge by the sirens, cars were heading toward them from various directions.

"WE CAN ALWAYS MAKE SURE," said Olofsson, driving past Clemens Square.

It was exactly six o'clock.

He let the car trundle slowly along Spool Street and all three of them looked in toward Peace Street.

"Great God Almighty!" exclaimed Mansson. "Isn't that a Volvo sedan sitting there!"

"He doesn't know she's left the apartment, of course," said Westerberg. "What do we do now?"

"Get some reinforcements," said Olofsson, switching on the radio. "SA Martin here. Over. SA Martin Four. Over."

"SA Martin Four here. Over."

"Olofsson here. All available cars to Clemens Square as soon as possible. No sirens. Over."

"No go. Car chase going on through town. Over."

"I must have men! We've got the Dog Ripper. Over."

"Okay. I'll reroute a couple of cars. Hell, and it's Christmas. Will two be enough? Over."

"What kind of car chase? Over."

"Don't know. Two cars tearing all over the place. Over."

"Okay. Send people as soon as poss. End."

"End."

Back to Spool Street after driving down Charles XII Street, then Charles XI Street and past the square, then he braked in where Peace Street crossed it.

"Westerberg, wait for them in the square. We'll go in from both ends of the street. Mansson, check that he's still there. You can walk slowly past as if you were on your way somewhere."

"Early service?"

"Where the hell you like. Take a discreet look into the car. But don't show any interest. Are you arm—what the hell's that?"

Sirens were wailing, clearly quite close.

"I told them no sirens!" said Olofsson. "What the hell are they playing at?"

Mansson looked behind the corner.

He came running back to the car.

"He's moving off!"

"Jump in! Westerberg, come back!"

Westerberg turned around in surprise, saw Olofsson waving at him and strode rapidly back toward the car.

"Run!" shouted Olofsson.

"What are we doing?" said Mansson.

"After him!" said Olofsson, accelerating even before Mansson had had time to shut the door.

The whole world seemed to be vibrating with the wail of sirens. They could hear nothing else. Clemens increased speed.

"It's not the ones I called up," said Olofsson. "It's those car maniacs."

"Bloody fine moment to start playing formula racing," muttered Mansson. "Shall we try forcing him to stop?"

"Haven't time."

Clemens drove up St. Laurence Street, onto All Saints Church Street, under the hospital bridge, on along Bishop Street, then took a sharp turn into the Botanical Gardens and onto Tome Street.

"Now what?"

They saw Clemen's car beginning to swerve. He had accelerated too fast and then tried braking too heavily on the turn into St. Anne's Street, so now his car was sliding toward the timbered building where the road curved.

The building was one of the most beautiful in town and the corner facing the church was cut off diagonally. It had originally been built as stables. Clemen's radiator hit the cutoff corner.

Mansson opened the door on his side and Olofsson saw he had a pistol in his hand.

"Steady now," he said, braking hard.

Clemens opened the car door and staggered out. He stood swaying back and forth, looking around, shaking his head and breathing heavily.

Mansson looked at him.

"Stand quite still," he said in a loud voice, raising his pistol.

Clemens did not seem to react, but then he suddenly raised his hand and Mansson instinctively threw himself down.

The jungle knife hissed over him and crashed into the wall of the house behind him.

Clemens started running down toward St. Anne's Street.

"Into the car!" cried Olofsson. "We'll drive after him."

"Better on foot!" shouted Mansson. "We can't get at him if he goes into the yards. But call up reinforcements!"

He set off after Clemens. It was slippery and difficult to run. He could hear steps behind him and for some reason turned his head, saw Westerberg and slipped. He was soon on his feet again.

They ran side by side.

With one leap Clemens was over the railings into the museum grounds.

Olofsson came up with the car and skidded to a halt.

"There are men all over the place," he said through the open window. "The car chase ended here. It was Holmberg after Palmer."

"Are they inside the museum area, too?" said Westerberg.

"That's what the duty man says. We must go in."

"Drive the car up onto the sidewalk," said Mansson, looking at the railings. "Put it right up against the railings and we can climb over them."

Olofsson did that and they climbed up to the roof of the car and were soon over the railings, landing softly in the snow on the other side.

PALMER HAD SWUNG OFF from Broad Street onto Paradise Street, turned off along St. Anne's Street and then right onto Noble Street. But two patrol cars had come in from the other end. The street was blocked.

Then Palmer had seen the open gate in the wall of the museum grounds. The gate was open for people going to the early service in Bosebo Church. He let the car run on, opened the door and jumped out, rolling over in the snow-covered street. Then he was on his feet again and through the gate.

He ran through the deep snow.

26

THE NET

THE SOUTH SWEDEN HISTORICAL SOCIETY had its beginnings in
an outing to the River Linderrod by a number of young
dialect researchers. They had hoped to record Skane lin-
guistic forms in the Huarod district. Their ambitions to pre-
serve dialects had been extended to attempts to conserve
material objects as well, and they gathered up a collection
that would otherwise have ended up in the hands of antique
dealers. Suddenly they found themselves the trustees of a
future museum. For this purpose, they founded the society
in 1882.

In the spirit of the founder of the Northern Museum in
Stockholm, Georg Karlin became the head of the Lund
Museum of Cultural History, which he ran with zeal and
foresight. Then in 1891, thanks to the acquisition of the site
in Noble Street, they had moved into the town center. Today the museum is an oasis of beauty and the best museum
of its kind in the country, situated on two sites on both sides
of Noble Street and consisting of as many as thirty buildings.

The past lives today in the museum. In the chancellery on
the corner of St. Anne's Street and Noble Street, in the
house called Locus Peccatorum, a student once killed a
fellow student and was beheaded a year later in 1830. There
are pools in the grounds that Per Henrik Ling had con-
structed to teach students the noble art of swimming. There
is everything inside the museum.

Outside this museum on Christmas morning were nine
police patrol cars and inside the walls were Gunnar Palmer,
Hans-Rudolf Clemens, four policemen from the Crime
Squad, twenty-two uniformed order police and two dog
handlers with their dogs.

Clemens was crouching down behind the ruins of the
Maria Minor Church, breathing deeply to try to calm him-

self. Then he ran crouching past Lindfors House and turned left just before the Manor House, the cellars of which held the museum's collection of silver.

Palmer was crouching behind the railings on the porch gallery of Dack Cottage, listening to the hymn singing from Bosebo Church and the crunching of snow under policemen's shoes.

He was thinking, they'll have to kill me before they get me. I must get away . . . there must be some way out.

But there was a policeman on guard at the gate facing Noble Street, and another man was posted over by the main gate, both armed with automatic pistols.

The remaining policemen were holding council by Dagg Cottage to decide on the best stage strategy. They had to encircle not just one man, but two unpredictable forces.

"We should rig up searchlights," suggested Mansson.

"We haven't time," said Olofsson. "Have you hurt your hand?"

"It's nothing," said Holmberg.

"What the hell have you been up to?"

"Can we talk about it later?"

"Look! There!" shouted one of the uniformed men. "Someone ran over there!"

He was pointing toward Thomander House. Between it and Berling House was a cobbled street that led right into the reconstructed town area.

"We'll barricade it!" said Olofsson.

This was soon done, for there were only two places where anyone could get out of the area, and no one could get inside the houses because they were all locked. If a window was broken, the sound would echo and tracks would bear witness if anyone had got inside.

It was still midwinter dark, torches burning at the open gate in Noble Street, and the path leading up to Bosebo Church lined with lighted candles.

But otherwise the whole area was dark, although the last remains of starlight and the full moon, together with the white snow, gave an impression that the darkness was lifting.

Two lines of portable searchlights were moving rhythmically in toward the area, methodically seeking, the light reflecting on the windows of the old houses of the nobility from Ystad and Lund; the Mayor's House, Schlyter House, Wahlbom House and Brahe House, the latter a copy of a medieval dwelling.

The houses had all been moved to the museum. Apart from the sight of them giving the viewer a sense of having taken a great leap backward in time, into a Christmas peace not even Christmas cards could achieve, the houses also functioned as exhibition spaces to illuminate the life of citizens of the past.

The great black mass of police uniforms appeared with their show of strength, sweeping the walls, alleys and hidden corners with the searchlights they were carrying. But they revealed no watchful shadow. Nowhere could they find what they were seeking.

Palmer had watched them hurrying over toward the group of houses, and now they were hidden from his view by the Manor House, once owned by Count Johan Christoffer Toll and now housing the collections of upper-class culture.

He could not go through the gate out onto Noble Street, as there was a guard there. But what about the other side?

Beyond the Macke village shop, beyond the village hall beside it, could he perhaps get over the thick hedge and railings there? He could escape along Little Tome Street, then in among the narrow streets between the low houses in the old town center, perhaps he could disappear. Disappear . . . to return and complete his task.

He mustn't get caught now.

Clemens had thrown himself down behind the steps to the Town Hall.

Now he would have to make use of his knowledge of commando tactics. He had to distract the enemy, make a mock maneuver and confuse them, worry them, but at the same time give them a sense of being at an advantage. He had learned to use that tactic to force the enemy into a position in which they were vulnerable and unprotected from attacks from the flanks.

It was a battle tactic, but it could be used as a means of retreat. Retreat was not very heroic, but it could be tactically useful, when circumstances had been weighed up and sober calculations made. Retreat was never heroic, but it could be used to gain time to build up plans for an attack. Battles were not won by ruthless and selfish sacrifice of one's only strength. The primary object was to judge the situation correctly and then carry out sensible measures.

How the hell did they know about me, he thought.

She must have alerted them, of course, though I told her what would happen if she asked the police for help.

Now he had to get away from there. The enemy had superior forces and he was not going to allow them to get him. Not going to get caught and interrogated again, he thought. Never again will I allow myself to be degraded like that.

But I'll come back, and then they'll experience terror they'll never forget.

And I'll get her. I'll get her. I'll get—

Now....

It was the right moment to break out, with the enemy's attention concentrated in another direction.

Cautiously and quite soundlessly, the dark-clad figure freed itself from the shadows.

My steps will crunch in the snow, but then they can't move soundlessly, either. I must keep my eyes open for hidden sharpshooters.

Hymn singing was pouring out loudly from the church like a sound filter over the darkness.

It was very dark behind Blekinge House. It would be all right if he could move without a sound.

Crouching low, he set off.

The snow crunched and swished under his feet, but did not seem to draw attention to him.

He walked calmly and slowly, putting his feet down carefully so as not to trip over anything.

He saw the hedge behind Onsjo Cottage, weighed down with heavy snow and revealing the railings.

There, he thought. Over and . . . then away.

Suddenly he heard steps quite close to him. He stiffened, standing quite still and listening, closing his eyes to be able to hear with all his senses.

Slow steps, as if dragging in the snow.

Crunch, crunch, crunch.

So there were police here, too.

He pressed himself against the cottage wall and peered out into the darkness.

Someone was coming, slowly but with a kind of bridled haste, holding a firearm in his hand.

Strange for a lone policeman to be creeping about.

Perhaps they had split up? The others were perhaps quite close? At the ready? Or perhaps reinforcements had arrived and the new men were looking here while the rest were still searching around the old houses?

He listened intently. He could hear no other steps. He opened his eyes and peered around. He could see nothing else. If there were more men here, then he would have heard more steps, too, wouldn't he?

Now the other man was hidden by the cottage there. Macke village shop, a timbered house with a porch gallery with lattice work of turned balusters.

He moved quickly across, hunching slightly in the compact darkness under the gallery, then looking carefully around the corner.

The man was creeping along the hedge, apparently studying something.

Is he trying to find out whether I've got over there? Why is he alone?

The man was keeping close to the hedge, at the same time coming nearer and nearer.

Clemens looked at the pistol in his hand.

I could take him by surprise, he thought. I could put him out of action before he knows what's happened. And then over and away. . . .

He crouched down, preparing.

He breathed deeply, concentrating on working up the oxygen in his blood, tensing his muscles as hard as he could, making his whole body rigid, his limbs, too. Then he drew a deep breath and held it, relaxing slowly as he emptied his lungs of air, letting it trickle slowly out through his nostrils.

Now his body was absolutely slack, his lungs empty.

Then he drew a deep breath and needed only four strides to get there.

BOSEBY CHURCH was built in 1652 from hewn timber and covered on the outside with shingles. In 1894 it had been moved to the museum and placed just inside the walls along Noble Street.

The church inside might appear gloomy and drab, but after sitting there for a while on the old wooden pews with their hard backs, people could experience the interplay and harmony in the contrasts between light and ancient dimness.

The altarpiece depicted the sacrament. Slightly away from the wall was a votive ship and in the pulpit was the minister.

Sleepy people were propped in the none too comfortable

pews listening to his words, some of them blinking to keep themselves awake, some dozing in the warmth from the candles, the sense of fellowship and their outdoor clothes.

"Christmas is a time of great joy," said the minister. "It is also a time of hope. Through the gift we receive, the greatest gift of all, we can hope that the light will come. This gift, His son, gives us the strength to believe in peace on earth and for mankind. Almost daily, almost every moment, we see human efforts failing to bring peace and happiness to mankind. But in their megalomania, these people forget to pray. For it is through prayer that the only grace is given to us, to humanity and to fellow members of mankind. Only through His grace—"

A shot rang out.

The minister started and several of the congregation looked around in confusion, but then the minister cleared his throat and went on, "It is through humble prayer, not heroic actions, that we can retain grace."

"CAME FROM OVER THERE!" shouted Mansson.

They were all outside Wahlbom House, conferring on the next step in the fine-tooth combing of the area.

They had established that there was no one there.

Another shot rang out.

They leaped into action.

It was slow work running through the snow as they cut across the lawns where the snow from the cleared paths had been heaped, but they struggled on.

It was like running in slow motion.

The noise they made was tremendous, then the sound of the organ inside the church surged out, followed by hymn singing as they ran.

They saw two men rolling about in the snow.

They heard them groaning and swearing.

A pistol was lying a short distance away from them.

Holmberg bent down and picked it up.

It was his own.

"Stop!" said Olofsson loudly.

The next moment, uniformed police were upon them, wrenching them apart. The dog handlers had to dig in their heels to stop their dogs joining in the fray.

They all stood there panting.

Five policemen were holding Clemens, who was kicking and struggling to get free. They twisted his arms behind his back, but he would not give in. He kicked out backward, striking a policeman in the groin with his heel, felling him in a bellow of pain. Then Clemens was given a hard blow in the stomach and again in the kidneys, until finally his head exploded as a blow struck him on the back of the neck, making his whole body slacken.

Two uniformed plicemen had twisted Palmer's arms up behind him so that he was bent right forward, and a third was holding onto him by the hair.

"Have you calmed down now?"

"Let go!"

"When you've calmed down."

"I—I have...."

The policeman let him go and Holmberg went up to him, signaling to the other two to loosen their grip.

Palmer straightened up and looked straight at Holmberg.

"I'll be back," he said. "You've won this time, but I'll be back. You can't shut me up forever."

Holmberg let his gun fall, then clenching his uninjured fist he struck Palmer in the face wtih all the strength he could muster.

Palmer was jerked free of the two policemen's grip and thrown backward. Holmberg leaped forward and grasped his coat by the lapels to drag him up, but Mansson and Olofsson intervened and managed to drag him off.

"Calm down, for Christ's sake!" snapped Olofsson.

Holmberg was breathing heavily, and he raised his injured hand to his face to wipe away the saliva from the corners of his mouth.

The towel had fallen off and then Olofsson saw his hand.

Blood was still trickling from the wound. Suddenly Martin's legs buckled and they had to catch him under the arms to prevent him falling to the ground.

Everyone was silent now.

There was no sound except the organ playing in the church.

"Happy Christmas," said Martin quietly.

27

IN THREE STAGES

NO ONE COULD UNDERSTAND how Gunnar Palmer had been able to put up any resistance against Hans-Rudolf Clemens. He himself could not explain it, but on the other hand, Clemens had laughed uncontrollably when he heard that Palmer was not a policeman.

Martin Holmberg was allowed to leave the hospital after treatment, and on Christmas Day Kerstin and the children went home. He was given sick leave and at last they could celebrate Christmas.

Seved Olofsson was in communication by telephone with Mansson in Lund to elucidate the shooting incident at a hotel in central Malmo. Before he went home he went down to the cells and looked at Palmer and Clemens through the spy holes in their doors, wondering whether they ought to have been taken to the hospital for treatment. Oh, well, under any circumstances they would soon be transferred to the criminal psychiatric clinic.

Leif Mansson and Lars Westerberg helped Olofsson put together the reports, and then they all went home.

The chief of police phoned Olofsson just as he arrived home, requesting a verbal report.

The duty officer at the station had the wretched job of explaining everything to all the journalists who telephoned. The evening papers the following day would come out as morning papers, which entailed guaranteed glaring placards, huge headlines and large sales of loose copies. The duty officer's task was wretched because he had not been on duty during that night.

Apart from the newspapers containing some of the events of the night over the next few days, they also included two striking contributions.

One was what might be called a minor storm of letters, all on the same subject: cruelty to animals.

One of the letter writers suggested that the guilty man should be castrated.

Another wrote:

Tears pour down my cheeks as I force myself to read about the madman who killed those dogs and that poor cat. At this moment, three lovely cats are lying on my sofa and my dog is sitting in front of me on the floor. One of the cats climbs up onto my knee, licks me, purrs, is happy, quite unaware of what I am reading. How can any human being be so callous? My heart is filled with hatred. It must feel good to torment a creature who cannot say in words how much *I* suffer, how much it hurts, the questioning eyes: why? Animals are worth as much as we are.

Another letter writer said:

How can some so-called human beings be so cruel? Are we human beings worth so much that these poor animals have to be tormented for our sake?

A man had written that, and another man wrote:

When I read about how he had killed those dogs and hanged the cat, I felt desperate, quite desperate. If I had seen that, I would have quite lost my senses. I would have rushed at whoever had done it and scratched his eyes out. And what is worse, I would have enjoyed doing it. I would be glad to go to prison for it.

These were random samples from the mass of letters, but it could be said with reasonable accuracy that most of them were on the same theme.

The other item was about the latest terrorist action.

On Wednesday the twenty-eighth, a terrorist group of five people had hijacked a Lufthansa plane on its way from Athens to Frankfurt. Apart from the crew there were a hundred and twelve people on board.

The hijackers had forced the plane down in Rome and it was now standing at the Leonardo da Vinci Airport. The hijackers were demanding the release of the remaining imprisoned members of the Baader-Meinhof gang and, in addition, nineteen million marks.

On Thursday the West German federal chancellor was kidnapped, despite the rigorous security measures surrounding him. On the same day newspapers and television stated that among the hijackers on board the Lufthansa plane was Herbert Klein, the terrorist who had shot his way out on the streets of Lund and inexplicably had managed to slip through the Security Police net. He was regarded as particularly dangerous and one of the new leaders in the West German terrorist movement.

The hijackers' deadline was the turn of the year. If their demands were not met, the German federal chancellor would be killed and the plane would be crashed onto one of the cities of western Europe.

At 2100 hours on New Year's Eve, the hijacked plane left the airport in Rome and set off on what the news reports called its "death flight." No one really believed the West German authorities would give in to the hijackers' demands, despite intervention from several governments in the West and appeals from the Pope, who also appealed to the terrorists.

At 2200 hours the children of the Holmberg family were asleep and Martin and Kerstin started seeing the New Year in on their own, armed with a bottle of Spanish red wine, paella, bread and five different kinds of cheese.

They avoided talking about the events of the Christmas holiday.

They did so mostly for the sake of the children, but also for their own sakes, hoping to put a distance between themselves and what had happened, so that they would be able to discuss it without fear.

· Both of them found it difficult to hate Palmer, and the children were delighted to have their father at home all day, although he did have his arm in bandages.

"Those poor people," said Kerstin, tucking her legs up beneath her on the sofa.

"What?" said Martin, taking a sip of his wine.

"Those people on board that plane, I mean. Do you really think the hijackers would crash the plane on some town?"

"I don't know. They usually mean their threats. But the point is whether the Germans will give in to their demands. Otherwise goodness knows what'll happen. . . ."

"What else could anyone do? Shoot down the plane?"

"No, they couldn't do that."

"No. But if the plane crashes onto a large town and lots of people are killed?"

"I know," said Martin. "But do we have to talk about it now? I've had just about enough terror for Christmas. We must forget it sometimes. Come and sit over here by me."

"You come over here...."

When they turned the radio on at five minutes to midnight to listen to the bells of Sweden's cathedrals ringing in the New Year, a special news bulletin was being read:

...as far as is known. The deadline is midnight, and if the hijackers are not to carry out their threat, the West German authorities must make an announcement soon. The German emergency council has been meeting all day, but as late as an hour ago no decision had been taken as to whether they should bow to the hijackers or not. If their demands are met, and I am just being handed a telegram...that says...that the hijacked plane is on its way...it is said to be on its way to Sweden! Over to our reporter for a direct report on the West German government's decision....

Martin switched off the radio.

"I can't stand listening to it," he said. "Let's make do with Lund Cathedral bells."

They opened the balcony door and stepped out into the snow in their garden.

Their garden was not large, but it was theirs and in the corner of it was its only tree, an apple tree that produced at least three hundred apples every other year, and only twenty or so in the alternate year.

The night was cold and clear, everything very still.

"Why did you switch off the radio?" said Kerstin.

"Why do you think?" he said, pulling her to him.

They stood holding onto each other, shivering a little.

"What can I do about violence and terrorism?" he whispered. "I'm nothing but a wretched little human being. On a night like this I don't want to think about it. It's New Year's Eve, after all."

He kissed her throat.

Then they heard the plane.

At first it was nothing but a subdued growling rumble. Then it came closer, the sound growing in strength and its wing lights visible in the sky. The plane made a wide swing below their area and then approached very low.

It was a very cold night, the snow glistening and glittering.

The plane thundered over the rooftops, then the cathedral bells struck twelve and it was 1978.

Then the whole sky seemed to explode as Sweden welcomed the New Year with fireworks.

The black night was transformed into a great crescendo of fiery color, crackling and banging and roaring, the sky exploding into every color man has found a name for.

And after flying in over Lund, the plane landed on time at the airport.

"I think I'll put on the radio," said Martin, feeling the cold. "There's bound to be a news bulletin."

"I'll go up to the children in case they've been woken by the New Year bangs. They might be scared. . . ."

They kissed each other a happy New Year, holding each other hard, neither wishing to be the first to let go.